101 PIECES OF ME

Veronica Bennett was an English lecturer for many years but now writes full time. Her interest in writing about early cinema was sparked by an article in a book about silent film actors. "I was struck by how very young the women were, though not the men," she says. "It seems that the seeds of movie culture, which even now demands youth and beauty from any aspiring actress, were sown right at the beginning. And sadly, so were the background stories we still read about every day, of betrayal, divorce, addiction. What would it be like, I wondered, to be a teenage girl living through the birth of celebrity culture?" Veronica lives in Middlesex with her husband, and has an adult son and daughter.

Books by the same author

Angelmonster

The Boy-free Zone

Cassandra's Sister

Fish Feet

Monkey

Shakespeare's Apprentice

Vice and Virtue

The Devil's Promise

For younger readers

Dandelion and Bobcat

The Poppy Love series

101 PIECES OF ME

VERONICA
BENNETT

WALKER
BOOKS

First published 2015 by Walker Books Ltd
87 Vauxhall Walk, London SE11 5HJ

2 4 6 8 10 9 7 5 3 1

Text © 2015 Veronica Bennett
Cover Photograph © Ilina Simeonova / Trevillion Images

The right of Veronica Bennett to be identified as author of this work has been asserted by her in accordance with the Copyright, Designs and Patents Act 1988.

This book has been typeset in M Bembo and Stuyvesant ICG.

Printed and bound in Great Britain by Clays Ltd, St Ives plc

British Library Cataloguing in Publication Data:
a catalogue record for this book is available from the British Library

ISBN 978-1-4063-5443-0

www.walker.co.uk

For Victoria Birt

OPENING REEL

LIGHTS

As I sit here on this balcony, watching the sea, I wonder what was real and what was imagined. Memory is like a dream. Like a film.

Some of it is documented, I suppose. The film itself (whose title, *Innocence,* is not without significance in this story) serves as proof that I was there, and did those things. But those reels of celluloid reflect more than just a two-dimensional image of me. Like them, I am a collection of pieces, almost but not quite the same as one another, progressing towards The End – those white words on the black screen. And as I go, I pass by the light that brings the film to life. Not the artificial light of a projector, but the real light of the sun, the bleached buildings, and this enormous sky.

Did you know that for each second that we live, twenty-four frames of film pass over the projector's beam? It doesn't sound like very many, does it? Even a hundred and one frames, the number that made up my very first appearance before the camera, only produce just over *four seconds* of moving picture.

What can you do in four seconds? Not much, you might think. But that is the time it took for my life to be changed. A hundred and one pieces of me, paraded before the world without my knowledge. Those four seconds of film took me apart, frame by frame. But now, here I am, together again. And frame by frame, I'll tell you the story.

I've always been a dreamer. In the days when I was scarcely taller than the hay grass, I was never a skinny child in a faded frock and pinafore, but the Princess of the Hay Field, or Queen of the Kingdom of the Cowshed, or wherever I had trailed my father that day. And later, when other village girls began to "walk out" with village boys, their whispered *he said – I said* accounts left me unmoved. I was waiting for something else to find me. Something not necessarily *better* than my family life in Haverth, since I loved both people and place, but definitely *different*. Something that might happen to the people I knew who didn't live in Haverth but lived inside my head. They were not farmers or shopkeepers or blacksmiths. They were the people in the films.

Ever since I had seen my first moving picture as a little girl in the church hall at Aberaeron, I had never stopped being amazed by the sight of real people moving on a flat white screen. One of Mam's favourite stories was of her own first visit to what she called the "kinema", years before. "We couldn't believe it!" she would say. "People were

11

running up to look behind the screen, trying to see where the pictures were coming from, and how they moved, just as if they were living. I didn't know whether to laugh or cry."

At the old "kinema", the people and horses in the film had walked jerkily, and unnaturally fast. The picture had flickered – brighter, then dimmer, then brighter again – as if illuminated by a guttering candle. It had seemed to struggle to stay within the bounds of the screen. "Bits of it would be on the wall," recalled Mam, "or on someone's face. It was funny, really, though marvellous as well. We were like children, watching those silly comic films that only lasted about five minutes, and clapping at the end, as if the people who made them could hear us!"

To me, even though the black and white made the world on the screen look so different from real life, it was still a miracle to see faraway places, sport and dancing and acrobatics, buildings and machines and animals. And what I loved best of all was that the pictures, or in my brother Frank's slang, "the flicks", were so *new*. They made you feel you were truly alive, striding through the twentieth century in a skirt shorter than any your mother or grandmother had worn, and with a head full of possibilities never before imagined.

Nowadays, the people on screen walk at the right speed, though the picture still flickers and jumps about a little, and even stops altogether sometimes. Frank, whose fascination for films leans more to the mechanical side than mine, met my questions about this with scorn: "What, do you think a film is shown by some sort of magic, girl? No, they are shown by a machine, and a machine can't see what it's doing, can it?"

I had to admit the truth of this. "So if the film stops, and the machine goes wrong, a man has to be there to see to it, then, has he?"

"Of course," said Frank, adding with authority, "he's called the projectionist." Then, with longing, "I think he's got the best job in the world."

Frank was two years older than me. We had always been companions, and unlike some brothers, he never excluded me from the things he was interested in. Though he was a farmer's son, he was a "war child", as I was myself. Born in the early years of the twentieth century, our lives had been changed by the Great War. Those four years stood like a monolith between the world of our parents and our own. The speed with which inventions were developing was almost alarming. Mr Reynolds, the headmaster, and Reverend Morris, the vicar, had telephones, and a public telephone box had even been installed on the quay at Aberaeron. People flew in aeroplanes. Faster and faster trains went to every part of Great Britain and all over Wales, to Anglesey in the North and Pembroke in the South, bringing things we had never had before. Bananas were the latest; Frank couldn't get enough of them.

Everything had changed. For generations, Freebodys had been tenant farmers, along with most of the families around us. But Frank did not see himself as a farmer, and I did not see myself as a farmer's wife. Greater, or at least new, things beckoned in this new, mechanized world. For Frank, especially. He liked films, but more than anything, he wanted to be a motor mechanic. And just like me, he dreamed. He would pretend to kick-start his battered old bicycle as if it were a motorcycle, and *vrmm-vrmm* his way down the lane. I laughed, but I understood.

When I was fifteen and Frank was seventeen, our parents took us to the Pier Pavilion Café in Haverth to see *The Bohemian Girl*, with Gladys Cooper and Ivor Novello. My da, who was fond of quoting poetry, told me on the way home that the film was "such stuff as dreams are made on". And he was quite right. It was from that day on that films became the centre of my dreams. Not baffling, disjointed night-time dreams, but the dreams of stolen moments when I was alone. Throwing feed to the hens, I ceased to be

Princess Sarah of the Hen Run and became Gladys Cooper or Gloria Swanson or Mary Pickford, scattering corn against a backdrop of American, not Welsh, mountains, my dress billowing around my legs, my hair in curls, to be noticed by Rudolph Valentino or Ronald Colman and swept into love and adventure. Most often, whether I was doing my chores or sitting on the gate, or reading, or walking to the shop, I dreamed of my favourite actress of all, the beautiful Lillian Hall-Davis.

Her name sounded upper-class, though I knew that before she became an actress in the films she had been an ordinary girl like me. When she was on the screen, I was transfixed by the way she moved and smiled and interacted with the hero. She was bold yet ladylike, sweet yet fiery, and so attractive that I never questioned that he would, of course, fall in love with her. I dreamed of her whenever I was bored, which was often. And I envied her. She had made her escape from a poor area of London and become a famous actress, a "star", as the film magazines said. I liked the handsome men in the films, but my imagination was filled with Lillian. And when no one was looking at me, I *was* her.

"But you're *always* an attendant!"

"Not this year, Flo."

Florence Price had been chosen as May Queen of Haverth. The previous year, it was Mary Trease. Even though I had been a May Queen attendant four times, I had no part to play in the May Day Parade of 1925 at all.

"Why not?" asked Florence.

I stopped threading privet branches round bits of wire, which was hurting my hands anyway.

"You know why not. Mr Reynolds said to give some other girls a turn."

"Mr Reynolds! He—"

"I know what he's like, but he's the headmaster and he chooses."

Florence sighed discontentedly. "I've always thought the vicar should choose, I have." When I did not reply, she sighed again, louder. "At this rate, you'll be too old to be the May Queen, ever."

"Flo, I'm eighteen, not eighty!"

She digested this, busy with the garland. "But I am seventeen. And last year, when you and Mary were both seventeen, he chose Mary." She looked up, her freckled face indignant. "It isn't fair!"

"No, it isn't," I agreed. "And it's especially unfair this year, considering."

"Oh, Sarah!" Florence was dismayed. "You mean the film, don't you?"

We were sitting in a front pew of the church, our feet surrounded by foliage. Privet, laurel and hawthorn had to be woven into strands to garland the cart that would carry the May Queen and her attendants through the village. It would be decorated with flowers first thing on Monday morning, and more flowers would be placed in the horses' bridles and the girls' hair. This year, thrillingly, it was rumoured that a moving picture was going to be made of the parade.

"I'm sure it's just gossip," I told Florence.

She shrugged. "Perhaps. But Mr Reynolds told Mr Hopkins the newsreel people want to come and film it. And Mr Hopkins told my da, and my da told us."

I tried to remember what I had seen on the newsreels at Aberaeron: a football match, a politician speaking on a platform (though as films had no sound, the content of his speech was written on the screen), fashionable women in London, an unemployed men's march in some European country. Would anyone watching a newsreel really want to see a May Day parade in a village in the middle of Wales?

"It does seem a pity," mused Florence as she worked. "Greenery looks so dull in the films, all grey and blurry. No one will see the beautiful colours of the flowers."

"But they'll see *you*, Flo!" I exclaimed. "You'll be up there looking lovely, and if it *does* get put on a newsreel, people all over Great Britain will see you and say to the person sitting next to them, 'There's a lovely girl, Mavis!' Or George, or whoever. Won't they?"

She grinned, her hands busy with the foliage but her blue eyes on my face. "Oh, Sarah! You and your films!"

Monday dawned misty, and by mid-morning a drizzle had set in.

"Good for the flowers," said Da, standing back to scrutinize the May Queen's cart. It was his job to drive it at the head of the parade. "I'll put some blossom in my cap, shall I?"

Frank was leaning against the gatepost, scowling.

"They'll never come and make a moving picture in this weather," he said. "Just when we had a chance to do something interesting, bloody Welsh weather goes and spoils it."

"You watch your tongue, Frank," said Da. He looked down at his muddy boots. "It'll be a while yet before it lets up, though. You girls had better watch your good shoes."

I was not sure I even wanted to *wear* my good shoes, or my best dress. Like Frank, I had been excited at the prospect of film-makers in the village. If they were not going to come, I wondered if I might put on my coat and boots, and keep dry. "Florence is going to need an umbrella," I told Da gloomily. "You'd better put some blossom on that, too."

"Cheer up, girl!" He slapped me lightly on the back. "At least you're not going to be up there in the rain in a thin dress! Maybe next year, eh?"

But by midday the rain had stopped, though the sky remained blank and greyish-white. I put on my dress and shoes, and my new hat. My reflection showed how narrow the close-fitting cloche hat made my face, and how large my eyes looked beneath its brim. I combed out some curls in front of my ears, but that made me look like a girl with side whiskers, so I tucked them back in. I touched my lips with the precious lipstick I had saved for and bought at the chemist in Aberaeron, then twisted it back down into its brass tube and stood back. There was little else I could do to make myself look more alluring; my dress was as fashionable as the pattern Mam had made it from would allow, my stockings were silk, my shoes, though second-hand, were not very worn, and newly polished. I thought I looked all right.

The street was full of puddles. I picked my way between them, my excitement growing. Men were setting up tables for the May Day supper, women were bringing baskets of food, children scampered everywhere, shrieking and getting in the way. There was no sign of Flo or her attendants, but I saw Mary Trease standing by the pump and waved to her. She smiled and came towards me, clutching her handbag. Her dress, of a pale lemon, silky material, fluttered around her knees.

"You look nice, Mary!" I told her. "What a pretty dress!"

"It belongs to my cousin down in Cardiff," she confessed. "But she's got lots of dresses. Sarah, do you think they'll come?"

"The film people? I hope so!"

"Let's you and I go and watch for them, shall we?"

I had nothing better to do, so I walked with Mary to where the road made its final bend between Aberaeron and Haverth. Our village was on a slight hill, so from here we could see all the way to the next rise in the road.

And as we watched, a motor car appeared, breasted the hill and putt-putted its way towards us. Mary caught my elbow. "There they are!"

The open motor car contained two men – strangers – wearing overcoats and hats.

Behind them, in the luggage compartment, was a large leather box surrounded by metal canisters and rods, cables and lamps: clearly, the paraphernalia of film-making.

The car swept by us into the village and stopped outside The Lamb and Flag. Mary and I hurried to join the crowd which immediately gathered around it, in time to hear Mr Reynolds calling for everyone to stand back and to see one of the men shake his hand. "Afternoon, sir," he said. "We spoke on the telephone. George Bunniford's the name, and this is my camera operator, Mr Preston. Now, where is the best vantage point for viewing the parade?"

Mary and I ran, stumbling a little in our unaccustomed heels, to the corner of the street outside the baker's. We knew the route the parade always followed. "Moll promised to keep me a place," Mary told me breathlessly. "And I'm sure there'll be room for you. You're only slim, not like *her*."

Mary's older sister Margaret, known as Moll, worked in the baker's, and took full advantage of the unsaleable cakes at the end of the day. She was actually a pretty girl, and evidently, considering the attention she received from boys, her curvaceous figure enhanced her beauty. Outside the baker's shop, which was closed today, of course, was a horse trough, over which Moll had had the presence of mind to lay a plank of wood. If the three of us stood on this make-shift grandstand and it held our weight, we would have a good view of the parade as it rounded the corner.

There was only just room for Mary and me. "Now, Sarah," she warned, "no jumping down there and trying to get in the picture, mind!"

"Couldn't we do that?" I asked her eagerly.

"No, of course not!"

"Why not?"

"It would spoil the parade, some daft girl running in, wouldn't it, Moll?"

Moll nodded gravely. "And if the parade is spoilt, they won't take the pictures, and we'll never see Haverth on the films. And it'll be all your fault, Sarah Freebody."

They were right; it was not our place to try to get into the picture on Florence's big day. But Mary and Moll had not been surprised that I wanted to. They knew me well; they knew my dreams.

"Look, Sarah, it's starting!"

I am ashamed to say I did not watch the parade. I missed Florence and the entire May Queen entourage; I missed the colliery band playing "Rhyfelgyrch Gwŷr Harlech" and the ponies with garlands round their necks and the Boy Scouts and the flag-waving and the cheering. I am sure it was all lovely, but to me it was not even there. I followed the movements of the camera operator, Mr Preston, and when I suspected the camera was turning towards me, I smiled at it. Mr Bunniford kept pointing out things he wanted Mr Preston to film, and I kept watching him. I so wanted to be in the newsreel! I wanted so very, very badly to be Lillian Hall Davis on a real screen, not just in my imagination!

Just as the May Queen passed, the sun came out. Seeing that the camera had turned straight to me, I waved. And it was on my face, not Florence's, that a sudden shaft of brilliant sunshine fell.

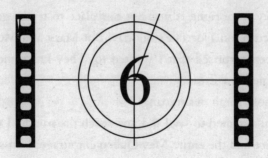

"Who? Here, give me that."

Da plucked the letter from my fingers and scanned it, frowning.

"George Bunniford," I repeated. "He's the man who came to make the newsreel film of the parade. You remember, Da, don't you?"

"Of course I remember." His frown lessened as he read on. "Well, I must say he's polite. Was he the tall one or the short one?"

"The short one," put in Frank, who was sitting on the stool by the back door, taking a long time to polish his boots. "The tall one was Preston, the camera operator. Bunniford was the director."

"*Mister* Bunniford to you, boy!" The corners of Da's mouth turned downwards, and he nodded approvingly at the page. "Director!"

"Can I go, then?" I asked him, as patiently as I could. "Can I go to Middlesex, like he says, and be in a film?"

"Whoa there, girl!" said Da. "He does not say anything

24

about you being in a film, now, does he?" He squinted at the writing and began to read aloud the paragraph that had almost stopped my heart. *"Your recent newsreel appearance was seen by the notable film producer and director, David Penn. He has requested that I invite you to attend a screen test at Shepperton Studios, Middlesex, as soon as is convenient."* Da looked at me over the top of the page. "And where might Middlesex be? I thought they made films in London."

"It's *near* London," said Frank. "It's where the film studios are, like it says."

Da did not look convinced. *"As you are under twenty-one years old,"* he read on, *"would you please seek permission from your parents. If they are agreeable, I would be grateful if they would sign the enclosed form and send it back to me at the above address. I remain, Miss Freebody, your humble servant, George Bunniford, Newsreel Director."*

"A screen test is a sort of audition," I ventured.

"I know what a screen test is." Da gestured with the letter towards Frank. "Living with you and this boy, with your film magazines and whatnot, Mam and I can't help knowing more than we want to about the whole daft business."

"It's not daft, Da!" Frank's flushed face looked up from his polishing. "If Sarah was in the films, we'd be rich! We could live in America, and I could have a motorcycle, or even a motor car!"

Da chuckled and tossed the letter back to me. "Ask Mam. She'll know what's best."

I went and kissed the top of his head. *Ask Mam* was half-way to *yes*.

"Hold the board a little higher, if you will, Miss Freebody. That's much better."

Click. Squawk.

"Thank you. You can give the board to Jeanette now. And while we're getting ready for the next photograph, would you show me your smile? That's right, smile as if you mean it!"

Click. Squawk.

"Now, would you turn your head to your left and lift your chin? Very nice."

Click. Squawk.

"And now the right side?"

Click. Squawk.

"Now, we're going to film you using the moving picture camera. Jeanette, would you hand the board back to Miss Freebody? Thank you."

I took the board, which said *SARAH FREEBODY,
D.O.B. 11.5.1907*, and pressed it to my chest. Behind it my
heart beat fast. I hoped the make-up that had been put on
my face would hide how much I was perspiring. The lights
that a young man had arranged in front of me were hot and
very bright. They were so bright, in fact, that the man
instructing me was invisible behind them. His attempts to
"put me at my ease", as he said, had failed. I had never felt
so unsure, so detached from real life, nor so excited.

"Ready?" came the disembodied voice.

"Yes, I believe so," I replied.

"Er, Miss Freebody, I was actually addressing the camera
operator."

"Oh, sorry!" Perhaps the make-up would conceal my
blush, too.

"We shall be taking moving pictures of you, my dear,"
continued the voice kindly, "so you must *move*. Do whatever you wish, letting us see you from every side, including
the back. Keep moving. And don't look at the camera."

The camera began to work, not clicking and squawking
like the one that had taken the still photographs, but making a loud whirring sound, like the wings of an enormous
bird. Of course I looked at it. Jeanette, who was perhaps ten
years older than me and wore large earrings and her hair in
a mass of waves, came and removed the board. I tried to
smile at her, but she took no notice.

The camera was still on. Without the board I felt naked,

though I was wearing a light dress, a pair of borrowed shoes and my best underwear.

"*Move*, Miss Freebody!" came the instruction. "And don't look at the camera!"

What did Lillian Hall-Davis do when the camera was on her? Into my mind came her face, flickering high above me on the screen, glowing with beauty and life. Copying her, as I had done so many times before, I took a few steps in a small circle, looking over my shoulder when I turned my back. I put my hands on my hips and swayed from side to side, trying not to imagine what I looked like. Maybe the invisible people behind the lights were smiling at my discomfiture. Anxiety swept over me; I bit my lip, recognizing dimly that I had forgotten to breathe. I took a big gasp of air, searching the blackness for any sign of someone who might tell me if what I was doing was acceptable, or stop me. But no one spoke. All I heard was the noise of the camera and my own rushing breath.

On and on it went. I seemed to have been standing in this wilderness of light for ages, moving my body awkwardly, like a child made to perform at a birthday party. Unlike such a child, though, I would not be indulged by my audience.

"Miss Freebody!" called a different voice from the darkness. "Dennis has asked you twice. If I ask you a third time, do you think you could possibly not look into the camera?"

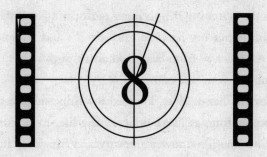

I could not see who had spoken. The voice was male, confident, well-modulated. The voice of a man in charge. I was relieved he had arrived. Surely he would soon tell the camera operator to stop filming. The imminent end to my ordeal gave me courage. "Where shall I look, then?" I asked.

"Look at *me*, if it would help." And the man stepped in front of the light.

He looked young, in his mid-twenties, and wore a suit and a thin moustache. I liked his face; it was boyish yet serious, with an expression of sympathy. "Just speak to me as if you had met me in the street," he told me. "Now, how did you travel to the studio today? By omnibus or train? Move your head a little, out of my shadow, and I want to see some animation in your face as we speak."

It was a great deal easier when there was someone to address. "By train," I said tilting my chin.

"Use your hands too," he said. "Did you come from Waterloo?"

"Yes, I did!" I had ceased to be myself. I was outside my

own body, watching this stranger performing as if she were in a film. I put my hands on my cheeks and widened my eyes. "All the way from Waterloo on a train!"

"And was your seat comfortable?"

I took my hands away, lowered my chin and gazed up at him, pretending, as I had done all my life, to be someone else. If no one liked my attempt to be a film star, at least I would have the comfort of knowing it was not Sarah Freebody who had made such an idiot of herself but a form-less, nameless product of her imagination. "Oh, it was splendidly comfortable, sir!" I assured the man.

"No need to call me sir, Miss Freebody." I felt his hand upon my wrist, and he turned to the darkness behind him. "Dennis, I believe we have enough."

"Cut!" said Dennis, and the noise of the camera stopped.

The man turned back to me and shook my hand. "Thank you very much. That was very nice. Please do stay for lunch, then a car will take you to the station."

It was over. The dead glass eye of the camera was no longer following me. I could feel perspiration trickling between my shoulder blades. Exhaustion spread through my body. "Could I have a glass of water?" I asked.

"Jeanette, water for Miss Freebody!" ordered Dennis.

I sat on a canvas chair and drank the water, watching Dennis and the man who had spoken to me standing in the corner, talking and nodding. I wondered who the man was. Dennis's superior, evidently, but how important? I was grateful to him, whoever he was. I had been floundering, and if he had not actually rescued me, he had given me the opportunity to rescue myself.

Back in Haverth, they would be waiting for my triumphant return. For a few days their expectations would remain. But then I would receive another letter from Mr Bunniford, which I would burn in the kitchen range before Mam or Da or Frank could get hold of it.

Crumple. Whoosh. Crackle. The end of my adventure.

But the letter I expected did not come. Instead, I received one on creamy paper embossed with gold. It was from David Penn Productions, of 110 Strand, London WC1, and it offered me employment as an actress in a film to be made at Shepperton Studios over the next few months. Again, a form had been enclosed for my parents to sign, and when they returned it, another, bigger collection of papers arrived. This was an official-looking contract, full of incomprehensible words.

Da took it to Mr Mord Williams, a lawyer friend in Aberystwyth whom he considered very learned. To my mind, anyone who did not know as much poetry as my father could not possibly be his superior in learning. But Mr Williams pronounced the contract legally sound, charging us half a crown for his services, and Da and I duly signed and returned it. Mam said the cream-and-gold letter was beautiful enough to frame, so she did exactly that and put it on the wall of my bedroom. By mid-June, I was on my way.

And I was no longer Sarah Freebody. Another letter had come from the production company telling me, to my delight, that I would be known as Clara Hope. And it was full of that hope that I stepped into the car that brought me from the Savoy in the Strand to another well-appointed hotel, this one in the country, by the Thames.

Jeanette, the woman who had been at my screen test, was waiting for me at the Thamesbank Hotel. "David Penn sent me," she explained, "to make sure you settle in all right, and that you have everything you need." When I asked if she was going to be my chaperone, she said, laughing, "I wouldn't call it that! But I am here if you need me. I do whatever David wants, and sometimes what he *doesn't* want!"

A few sleepless hours later, in the mist of a summer dawn, a different car collected me and delivered me to Shepperton Studios. And my new life began.

I will try to describe what took place during those first few days at Shepperton, as I remember it happening, in the right order. But films, like the dreams my father's poet compared them to, do not lend themselves to order. Time in dreams shifts backwards and forwards, and images come and go, and so it is with the making of a film. Unfamiliar sights, people, language and experiences tumbled like a kaleidoscope, and dazzled me.

As soon as I entered the studio on that first day, the man whose banal questions about my train journey had encouraged me during my screen test strode towards me, extending his right hand with an expectant look. "Miss Hope? I am David Penn."

"Oh!" I shook his hand. "So that was *you*!"

"You seem surprised," he said, smiling.

"Um…" I was embarrassed, but found myself so struck by his appearance that I could not look away. I had seen him before, of course, but I had not seen his smile before. It covered his entire face, from his eyelashes to his ears,

33

from his hairline to his moustache. He carried the fact that he was the best-looking man in the room with ease, from the collar of the jacket draped over his shoulders to the tips of his brogues. For the second time, I was charmed by his attention. "I *am* a little surprised," I admitted. "You are such an important person, I—"

"And you are not?"

My embarrassment increased. I did not know what to say.

"Very well," he said, "I will cease making you uncomfortable, and instead I will welcome you most humbly to David Penn Productions and Shepperton Studios. I trust you are being well taken care of?"

"Oh, yes! Very well, thank you."

"Splendid." He looked around the studio, then turned back to me. "Miss Hope, I promise you, by the time a few days have passed, you will feel you have been doing this your whole life. I am convinced you are a natural actress."

"I am glad you think so," I told him shyly. "I have no such confidence myself. And please, call me…" – I hesitated; it was the first time I had uttered my new name to anyone – "Clara."

"Of course, and you must call me David," he said quickly. "Now, Maria will show you to your dressing room, and someone will bring you whatever you would like to eat and drink, and then you will have your costume fitted and your hair and make-up done. We will be taking some more test shots, just to see how you look. And there will be a script conference with Aidan when he arrives. You have read the script, have you not?"

I nodded. The story involved my character, Eloise, a serving girl, falling in love with an aristocrat during the French Revolution. The aristocrat, Charles de Montfort, was beheaded in the end. "Who is Aidan?" I asked tentatively.

"It is not his real name," said David. "I believe it is Irish, though he is not. He probably considers it exotic. You will get to know him quite well, my dear. He is playing de Montfort, your leading man."

My leading man. Doubt and panic rose, silencing me. I could only smile faintly as David beckoned to Maria, who greeted me cheerfully. She was a gaunt woman of about forty, with a calm demeanour and a knowledgeable air. She had, I was immediately convinced, the measure of me and everyone else. "Will you come with me, Miss Hope?" she asked pleasantly.

"Oh please, do call me—"

"To Maria, and Jeanette, and Dennis, and the rest of the film crew," David interrupted, "you are Miss Hope."

He said it kindly, but as I followed Maria through a maze of corridors I felt a fool. I *was* a fool to think I could do any of the things these people expected me to do. Nausea gripped me suddenly. I quickened my pace. "Please, where is the ladies' room?" I asked Maria urgently. "I think I'm going to be sick."

Maria waited, ready to help but not fussing, while I retched. But there was nothing in my stomach. "You'd better eat something," she said. "Come and sit down, and take some deep breaths. You'll soon be all right."

Someone brought me a cup of tea and some toast, and then Maria and other members of the costume and make-up team worked on me for a long time, until David was satisfied that they had transformed me into an eighteenth-century French servant. I gazed in astonishment at my reflection. My eyes were enlarged by make-up, my hair thickened by false curls, and my figure was unrecognizably enhanced by a corset under flowing sleeves and a lace apron.

When I walked onto the film set I no longer felt sick. I was Clara Hope in the guise of Eloise. I did not quail at the thought of Mam and Da and Frank, and Mary and Flo, and everyone else in Haverth seeing me on the screen. They would not see me. They would see an actress.

"Clara, you look divine!" exclaimed David. "Aidan, where are you? Here is your Eloise!"

A man in eighteenth-century jacket, breeches and stockings picked his way through the tangle of wires on the studio floor. He was shorter than David, though slim and well-made, with an actor's expressive eyes. Incongruously, the head that appeared from the collar of his lace-trimmed shirt sported short, twentieth-century hair and a tweed driving cap. "Got a cigarette?" he asked.

In Haverth, only men smoked. "No, I'm afraid not," I told him.

"So…" He scrutinized me as attentively as if I were a horse he was considering buying. His expression was sombre; under the peak of the cap he was frowning deeply. "You are Clara Hope and I am Aidan Tobias. I'm really Allan Turbin. Who are you?"

"Shut up, Aidan, and let's get started," said David. "Harry, Kitty, Bernard, get moving. I want Aidan and Clara sitting on this sofa. Maria, where's Mr Tobias' wig?"

David had taken off his jacket. In shirt sleeves and braces, he strode to his chair, sat down decisively and crossed his legs. I looked at him carefully. He was wearing checked socks and brown and white shoes of a type I had never seen before. Then, embarrassed, I turned away before he could catch me looking at him.

He was immediately surrounded by Dennis, Jeanette and people who I assumed must be Harry, Kitty and Bernard. Jeanette gave me an encouraging smile. Aidan and I sat down on the brocade sofa in front of French windows that looked out on nothing but a "flat", as the temporary walls around the set were called. While David issued instructions, Aidan muttered to me.

"I'm *indescribably* fed up with being cast in historical romances."

I did not reply.

"Don't you think it's outrageous that David Penn Productions is making yet *another* one?"

Again, I said nothing.

"I'm sure this wig they've given me is full of bugs."

I was silent.

"Are you quite certain you don't have a cigarette?"

"Please," I whispered at last, "had we not better be quiet?"

"Why? Whatever we say must be a damned sight better than this script."

"Please…"

"What are you doing here, anyway?" His eyes narrowed.

"You are very young. Why aren't you at home with your mother, living a decent life?"

I was unsure how to respond. He was impertinent, but he was my leading man, and I did not wish to be rude to him. "I am perfectly happy here, thank you. I have been given a wonderful opportunity any girl would envy me for. Now please, let us get to work."

"Ah." He pursed his lips and shook his head. "I see. Very young. But not for long, Miss Clara Hope."

His condescension irritated me. "What do you mean?"

But he chose not to reply, and soon Dennis called us to order, and the test shooting of my very first scene began.

The lights were hot; perspiration was evident beneath Aidan Tobias' make-up, and my armpits and waist felt damp beneath my heavy costume. Perhaps, among all the innovations of the twentieth century, women's light clothing was the truly revolutionary one. The thought made me smile.

"Lovely smile, Miss Hope, but unnecessary," called Dennis. "This is only a lighting test."

Admonished, I straightened my face.

"Oh, come on, Dennis, it's her first day, don't y'know." Aidan seemed to be exaggerating his upper-class drawl. "Grant the poor girl a nervous grin if she wants one, can't you?"

"I am not nervous," I told him coldly. "Not in the least."

"Why were you smiling, then?"

"That has nothing to do with you," I said, gathering courage. "And since it was unnecessary anyway, as Dennis says, it is not worth discussing."

He stood back and looked at me approvingly. "You're quite plucky, aren't you?"

"And you are very rude."

"Er ... Aidan, would you get back into shot?" asked Dennis plaintively. "I don't want this to take longer than absolutely necessary."

The test filming *did* seem to take a long time. David scrutinized us closely, sometimes looking through the camera, sometimes not, requesting that Maria change the make-up under my eyes and make Aidan's eyebrows "more sardonic". Although he complied without complaint with requests to turn, look up, look down, move to a marked spot, Aidan appeared bored.

"Can we have a clinch? See what you two look like together?" asked David. He turned to Dennis. "What do you think? On the sofa, or by the window?"

Dennis pursed his lips. "Let's test a shot in front of the window, for the lighting."

Aidan and I were positioned in front of the window, which wasn't a real window, of course. Lit from behind, we also had to be lit from the front or our faces would be in shadow. We waited while lights were adjusted, me patiently, my leading man less so.

"God, this is tedious!" He wiped his forehead with the cuff of his shirt. "When will they invent a light that isn't hot as well as bright? It must be ninety degrees in here."

"I'm sure it isn't," I said calmly. "And anyway, you must be used to it."

He nodded moodily. "Too damned used to it, that's the trouble."

"Righty-ho!" came the call from the man whose name was Harry. I remained mystified by what his actual job was, though it seemed important. David and Dennis discussed each test with him before they filmed it, and it was Harry's confirmation that everything was ready that started the filming.

"Now get together, you two," instructed David. "You don't have to look as if you mean it, but for Christ's sake, Aidan, do try not to yawn."

We stood close together, and Aidan put his arms around me. I had been expecting this, since we were playing lovers, and David had asked for a "clinch", which every filmgoer knew meant a passionate embrace. But I did not expect Aidan's hand to go to the back of my head and draw my face so close our cheeks were touching. His skin felt sweaty and sticky; I could smell smoke on his breath. My body felt tense, and weighted by my costume. It was not a passionate embrace.

David sighed. "Fine. Look into the camera, both of you."

We did so, cheek to cheek.

"Look at each other."

We drew apart, still with our arms around each other. I gazed into dark eyes, outlined with make-up but expressionless. Aidan's nose and cheekbones, I noticed, were prominent. His face was that bony English type so sought-after by film directors. Not winningly open and handsome like David's, but striking, especially in profile.

"All right." Another sigh from David. "I suppose that will do. Maria, powder please!"

Maria dusted the powder puff over both our faces. When she saw the make-up smear Aidan had left on his cuff, she did not say anything but gave him a weary look. When we were powdered to his satisfaction, David took my hand and led me to the little sofa.

"Gorgeous, Clara," he said. "Now, let's try a rehearsal."

By the time we had finished the rehearsal my head ached and my feet were balls of fire.

"Maria, I think these shoes are too tight," I ventured awkwardly.

"New shoes for Miss Hope!" called Dennis, though I had not addressed him.

"Dennis orders Maria about, not you," whispered Aidan in my ear. "It gives him something to do."

I thought Dennis, and everyone else who worked in the studio, had plenty to do. If I squinted, the scene before me turned into a swimming mass of colours: the dark shapes of the cameras, the huge lights above, the cables on the floor as thick as elephants' trunks, the illuminated eighteenth-century stage where I sat and the muted twentieth-century shadows where those who were watching me lurked. Their faces looked ghostly as they worked in the gloom – talking, arguing, occasionally laughing, jotting things down, operating machines of which I had no knowledge, examining those same machines when they did not work properly, and cursing casually, not always under their breath.

However, my own job seemed clear. I had to turn up on time every morning, do as David or Dennis requested and learn, by process of trial and error, how to act in a film. Everything was so new and complicated. I was determined to be careful about what I said and to whom, and to hold my tongue unless spoken to.

Aidan Tobias, however, had no such scruples. He said whatever he liked. I wondered if he knew how lucky he was to be in films and not have to work on a farm or in a factory or an office like most young men. He did not seem to like being an actor, and I found that baffling.

The rehearsals that day were exhausting. I was glad I was not acting in the theatre, where I would have had to project my voice as well. But because the films were silent, we could say the lines as loudly or as softly, as well or badly, as we wanted. Eager to please, I stuck valiantly to the script I knew the audience would never hear. The words helped me to understand what my face and body were supposed to be showing the viewers of the film: love, fear, happiness – whatever David demanded. But Aidan was so easily bored, and so experienced, that he no longer needed such an anchor. He would sail carelessly into improvisation, jokiness and sometimes downright rudeness, in his own words instead of the scripted ones. Everyone would laugh, the scene would be ruined and we would have to do it again.

Rehearsals went on, hour after hour. I had no clear sense of how much time passed: day might as well be night. The studios were a collection of shed-like buildings on the edge of a small town near the Thames, but once inside them I felt as if I might as well be underground. There were no windows; interior and exterior light had to be created by electric arc lamps strung from the invisible ceiling, and windy or misty conditions created by large fans operated by the technical staff. Everyone seemed to drink coffee, but I preferred tea. "Cup of tea for Miss Hope!" became Dennis's refrain that first day. David never drank coffee or tea, only water. And Aidan accompanied his coffee with a swig of something from a hip flask he kept in his jacket pocket.

David chided him. "Inseparable from that thing, aren't you? Like a baby and its bottle."

"You'd drink, too, if you had to put up with a director whose childishness is more evident than any baby's," Aidan retorted. "Light me a fag, will you, Jeannie?"

Jeanette did not obey; smoking on the film set was strictly forbidden. But Aidan never gave up his quest to irritate everyone, though it was obvious that all he did was bore them. When I asked Maria why he did it, she shrugged and said, "That's not for me to say, Miss Hope. Mr Tobias is a lovely actor, even when … you know, he's had a tipple, and that's what matters, I suppose."

Jeanette did not seem to consider it necessary to introduce me to the technicians. They ignored me as they went about their work. But to their surprise, and possibly their embarrassment, I could not ignore them.

"And you are…?" I said to the man in the cap while he was adjusting a lamp.

"Cinematographer, Miss Hope."

"And what is your name?"

"Harry, Miss Hope."

"And what does a cinematographer do?"

Blank look. "Er … the moving pictures. I'm in charge of the photographing."

Blank look from me.

"Er … the cameras, like. I keep them working and sort out the lighting, and the effects, and how it all looks through the camera. You know, get it all how Mr Penn wants."

I held out my hand for him to shake. "Well, I'm very pleased to meet you, Harry."

While I was drinking tea during a break, I tried the same

tactic on the boy who was winding cables in the corner. "And you are…?"

"Me?" His face was scarlet. "Grip, Miss Hope."

"Grip? Your name is Grip, you mean?"

"No, miss. My job. I'm a grip. Me and all them others, we're the grips," he said, nodding towards a group of five or six men, also on their tea break, playing cards on a box.

"And your name is…?"

"Alfie, miss."

"And what do you, er, grip, Alfie?"

Met by his silent bewilderment, I tried again. "Look, I am very new and want to find things out. I mean, why are you called a grip?"

His embarrassment increased. "Don't know, miss."

"Well, what do you do?" I asked patiently.

"We're like stage hands. We do what the gaffer tells us."

The gaffer? I felt defeated. "Very well, Alfie, thank you. Now, I had better let you get back to work."

One person never seemed to have a break. The film set was haunted by a young woman with fashionably bobbed hair, who scribbled constantly on a notepad. Her eyes darted everywhere; she missed nothing, and when Aidan and I left the set she photographed it solemnly, from several directions, with a still camera. I could not fathom what she was doing.

She was friendly towards Maria, Harry, Dennis and Jeanette, so when a suitable moment arrived near the end of the day, I approached her. "And you are...?"

Her eyebrows shot into her fringe. "I'm Kitty!"

"And what is your job, Kitty?"

"Continuity, Miss Hope."

"Continuity?"

She lowered her notepad and showed it to me. "Well, you see, I make sure everything's exactly the same on the set for the next time."

This meant little to me. "Um ... the next time?"

"For going back over the scene. If you've got your hand

48

under your chin when the camera films you from the front, Miss Hope, you've got to have it there when it films you from the back, and that could be on a different day altogether. If I didn't note it down and take a photograph, we'd be forever going over bits of film and taking ages, and Mr Penn wouldn't be pleased!"

"Oh, I see." I did not, really. A different day altogether?

"And Dennis!" she added in a rush. "He's a stickler for continuity!"

I seized this opportunity. "Tell me, Kitty, what is Dennis's job, exactly?"

"Why, Miss Hope" – she was trying to hide her astonishment – "Dennis is the AD. The Assistant Director."

"And Mr Penn is the Director?"

"Yes, and the Producer, too. He's the big boss, and Dennis is our … immediate boss."

"Oh." I pondered for a moment. "I thought *Jeanette* was Mr Penn's assistant."

Kitty was beginning to look uncomfortable. "She is. She looks after him, like a secretary, and you know, manages everyone."

"And Maria?"

"She's the Wardrobe Mistress. The girls in costume and make-up are under her."

"And you are under Dennis?"

She nodded. "And Harry too. They work together, under Mr Penn."

49

"And the grips work under them, too?"

"That's right." She waited politely in case I had any more questions, then, tucking her notepad under her arm, she gave a nervous nod and made her escape.

I sighed. The business of film-making appeared to have class divisions as complicated as those of Britain itself. From the King to the vagabond tramping the lanes of Wales, everyone had their place, and so it seemed at Shepperton. With so many social tripwires all around me, how could I possibly stay on my feet?

"You look miserable," said a voice at my elbow. "Justifiably, I'm sure."

It was Aidan. In his drawn face I saw my own exhaustion. "Not miserable," I told him, "but tired."

"Hah! We've hardly done anything today, with only you and me here!"

He could tell from my expression that I did not know what he meant, and smiled without humour. "I suggest you go and look at the call list Jeanette's put up. Tomorrow the rest of the cast of this ghastly enterprise will turn up for work, and believe me they're a pretty rum crew. I've worked with a couple of them before. You'd better watch your step."

I took little notice of his words. Whatever happened tomorrow, I was ready for it. Shepperton might be a place as far removed from Haverth as fairyland but, bewildered as I still was, I had realized two things. First, my contract would not allow me to get away from these people until we had completed the film, even if I wanted to. And second, I did not want to. Everything I had dared to imagine as I sat on the farm gate was here. Modern surroundings and modern people. Beautiful things and beautiful people. Knowledge, worldliness, power, achievement, creativity – all showered with the glamorous light of the cinema screen. I knew I stood on the threshold of a shadowy place that would present unimagined challenges. But I was ready for them. Now I was here, I wanted to stay in fairyland.

The call list was a typewritten piece of paper pinned to a noticeboard outside the dressing rooms. It was, as Aidan had explained, a list of the actors who had been called for filming the next day. I had assumed there would be more leading actors than there actually were. Besides Aidan's and my own, there were only four main parts: the Comte de Montford's uncle, a revolutionary leader, his mistress and her maid.

"How can a film about the French Revolution have so

few people in it?" I asked Jeanette, who was standing at the call list, frowning. I knew all the action did not take place in one room, like a stage play; I had read the script. So where was everyone else?

"They'll use extras," she told me. "You know, people from a theatrical agency who do things like being peasants, Parisians, soldiers and sailors and so on, to make it look realistic. Tomorrow we're just doing scenes with you six – or five, as it turns out." She took a pen from behind her ear and crossed out someone called Simona Vincenza. "Miss Vincenza's agent telephoned last night to say she can't get here until Thursday. Something about an aeroplane. So that puts the whole schedule out. David'll be livid."

"Is she the maid or the mistress?" I asked.

Jeanette laughed so loudly and suddenly that it made me jump. She put her hand up apologetically. "Sorry, but the thought of Miss Vincenza playing a maid is such a hoot! I must tell Harry."

"Um…" I tried not to look as embarrassed as I felt. "Please don't, if that's all right, Jeanette."

She stopped smiling and regarded me with interest. Understanding came into her eyes. "Oh … very well, of course I won't. You can't know what Miss Vincenza's like, after all."

"Thank you."

She was embarrassed that she had considered gossiping about my ignorance. She put her head down so that her hair

52

fell over her face, and busied herself with putting the pen away in the pocket of her dress. "See you tomorrow, then!" she said brightly, and disappeared down the corridor.

My cheeks were still pink when I returned to the dressing room. Maria gave me a curious look but said nothing. I refused Jeanette's offer to accompany me to dinner and ordered it in my room instead. Unable to fight down my nervousness, I ate very little, made a sketchy, shivery toilette in the hotel bathroom, and went to bed.

I lay awake for a long time, planning not only my own conduct in front of the rest of the cast but also how to deal with Aidan Tobias. I dreaded having to do scenes again and again because he had wrecked them. I went over and over things to say and ways to behave that might discourage him. I toyed with the idea of throwing a tantrum, leading-lady style, threatening to walk off the set unless he behaved himself. But I soon dismissed this. Aidan losing his job did not worry me; losing my own certainly did. And it was with this worrying thought squeezing my brain that I eventually fell asleep.

Today was the first day of filming. Not a lighting or camera test, but the real thing. Tonight, there would exist a length of exposed film showing me – or at least someone who looked a bit like me – acting in her very first moving picture. The nerves I had endured last night were gradually replaced by relief that we were getting on with it at last. And as the day went on, the pieces of the kaleidoscope that had so baffled me began to settle.

We did the scene we had rehearsed yesterday. The set and lights were checked, Aidan and I "blocked" the scene, making our moves without acting or speaking, and the lights were adjusted until Harry, behind the camera, was satisfied. Then he shouted, "Set!" which meant, "Everyone on the set who shouldn't be, clear off!"

David, who was such an exacting director that it had taken ages to get the scene set up to his liking, eventually called "Roll camera!" and Harry started the camera and called back, "Rolling!" Then Dennis called for the clapperboard.

The contraption known as the clapperboard seemed to

me old-fashioned. The primitive wooden board with a hinged top seemed to have no place in this modern, electrified studio. It did not take me long, however, to realize it was the most important piece of equipment of all. Without it, it would be impossible to make a film.

The clapper boy, as he was called (though he was not a boy at all, but a man called Bernard who was at least forty), was the clapperboard's master. As soon as the camera started rolling, he put the board in front of the lens and "clapped" the hinged part down to signify that the scene was being filmed. Only then did David call "Action!" and the filming properly began. After each scene, Bernard bore the clapperboard away with a proprietary action, rubbed off the scene number, and chalked on the next with a piece of chalk he wore on a thin chain around his neck. Sometimes he would have to wait a long time before he could do this, but it was his job and no one else's. Ever.

I was thrilled that at last I understood. When Frank threw his leg over his bicycle or tossed a bale of hay onto the stack or clattered down the stairs in his nailed boots, he would shout, "Lights, camera, action!" Now, I could tell him exactly how those three elements combined to film the scene. My next letter to him would be a long one.

As I set this down all these months later, it seems as banal and repetitive as Aidan considered the business of making a film. But then it was the most exciting thing imaginable. That moment when the clapperboard went "smack!" and

I put my actress's face on was like an alarm clock going off. "Get up, Clara Hope," it said, "and do what – astonishingly – you get paid to do!"

Furthermore, to my inexpressible relief, Harry's call of "Rolling!" seemed to work magic on Aidan. He kept his head down while Bernard slapped the clapperboard shut. But then his head came up, and a miracle took place.

He began to act.

There was a light in his face that had not been there in rehearsals; a quickness, as if his internal battery had been switched on. Not only did he not improvise or giggle, he played the part with such professionalism that I forgot he was Aidan and started to believe he was de Montford. It was suddenly much easier to be Eloise.

"Marvellous! Perfect!" exclaimed David when the take was over. He came towards me, applauding, his face pink with excitement. "Clara!" His voice was almost a shriek. "That was absolutely wonderful. You're a natural, just like I said." I was sitting down; he put his hand on my shoulder in a fatherly way. "Now, why did you not show us this in rehearsal? I've been worried sick that you wouldn't do!"

"So have I," I confessed. "But … I don't know, it just felt so different to know it's a real performance that people are actually going to see."

I did not add that the sudden attention that Aidan had brought to his own performance had given mine life. David squeezed my shoulder. "We're going to do another take,

56

and we don't know yet which we'll use, so you've got to give it everything this time as well, all right?"

I nodded, happy in the expectation that Aidan would also "give it everything". It was his ability to do this, I realized, that must show in screen tests and get him parts. "Natural" or not, I must seem to Aidan Tobias an amateur who had got the role by means of mere luck. In contrast, he was an actor of rare ability, much more deserving of praise than I. Yet David had pointedly, publicly ignored him.

Robert Palliser, a middle-aged actor who was playing de Montfort's uncle, was always very kind to me. Off-screen he wore thick glasses, and was very amiable, like a real uncle. "Are you all right, my dear?" he asked me that day at the first break. "You're so young, you must be absolutely floored by all this."

"Yes, I am," I confessed. Then, so as not to seem too idiotic, I added, "Well, a bit."

"Much of what goes on must seem unfathomable."

"It does, rather," I said. "Though I've managed to find out that Harry is the cinematographer, and Kitty is the continuity girl, and Alfie is one of the gropes."

Robert Palliser's small pink mouth fell open.

"Oh! Sorry, I mean *grips*. The boys who shift things around."

"Ah." The pink mouth expanded in a surprisingly pleasant smile. "Well, you've done better than I did when I first started in this business. I wouldn't say boo to a goose." He considered. "But then, I was a mere boy, quite untried. You seem very poised for one so young."

"Aidan says I'm plucky."

He looked at me from under lowered eyelashes, his expression unreadable. "Well, Aidan has his own view of the world, and that's a fact. Tell me, is your mother with you?"

"No. She is needed at home. She … er … helps my father in his work." I looked at him, feeling uncertain. "Eighteen is old enough to be by oneself, though, don't you think?"

"Of course." He patted my hand. "And naturally you'll see your family soon, will you not? Why not invite them to tour the studios?"

I could not answer. Surprise at his suggestion and a sudden closing of my throat prevented me.

"You are missing them, aren't you?" he asked softly.

Swallowing, I nodded. "My brother – his name's Frank – he'd love to come here," I continued, but then I had to stop again. An inexplicable wave of longing to be back in

Haverth had buried me. I strove to compose myself. "Um … I write to them, and they write to me," I told him. "That will have to do for now, I think."

"Dear girl!" exclaimed Robert. "Would you like to sit down?"

"Please don't concern yourself," I said, sniffing a little. "I am quite all right."

At that moment the actor playing the revolutionary leader passed. Robert caught his sleeve. "Ah, Godfrey! Come and join me and the delightful Clara Hope, our young star."

Godfrey Claymore, a rangy Scot with a face more aristocratic than a revolutionary leader perhaps ought to have, gave me a sympathetic smile. "Hello, darling," he said, which flattered me until I discovered that this was what he called everyone, even the men. "In at the deep end? Robbie here will always pull you out when you need it, you know. He's wonderful with the ladies." He and Robert exchanged a look. "And talking of ladies," continued Godfrey, "be grateful, Clara darling, you're not contending with La Vincenza quite yet." He sucked in air through his teeth. "Even Robbie can't deal with *her*!"

I was still trying to recover and did not reply. Godfrey scrutinized me for a moment, then said, "Toodle-oo!", waved happily and melted away. Robert Palliser giggled. "My dear, old Godfrey may be a bit of a gossip, but he's quite right. If you feel all at sea, you only have to ask and we'll haul you out." He gestured with the script he held. "Now, to work. We're on next. Do you want to go through this?"

"Aidan, for the last time!"

It was the end of another long day of rehearsals. David had spent the morning in a meeting with the people he called his "money men". He had returned to the set at lunchtime, his normally open expression obscured by anxiety, and had been grumpy all afternoon. By the time six o'clock came we were all exhausted. Aidan, perhaps hoping to lift the mood, had begun to ignore the script and improvise, and David had lost patience. "Are you intent upon sabotaging this film entirely?" he demanded. "Or are you merely trying to stop us finishing it on time?"

Aidan was kneeling on the floor. We were rehearsing the scene where he declares his love for Eloise, who was sitting on a kitchen chair with Maria adjusting her skirts. He stood up wearily and shrugged. "Do you want me to tell you how little I care?"

David's lips got very thin. "I'm warning you…"

But Aidan spoke over him. "*What* are you warning me? That filming will run over schedule and cost more than you have told those money-grabbing self-abusers you call your investors? That is your concern, dear David, not mine."

I did not know what a self-abuser was, but judging by David's reaction, it was a not inconsiderable insult to the money men. He stared at Aidan, and the muscles in his face seemed to loosen, as if he was no longer controlling them. His voice was cold. "And what *is* your concern, *dear Aidan*?"

Aidan strolled across the floor to the area behind the cameras, where his jacket was hanging over the back of a chair. From one of its pockets he took a pack of cigarettes and a box of matches. Knowing that smoking was forbidden on the set, I watched in trepidation. Unhurried, Aidan lit up and took the first puff with satisfaction. "My concern," he announced to the silent, waiting studio, "is this. Where am I going to get drunk tonight, and who is going to join me? Dennis, how about you? Shall we descend upon Claridges, or the Café Royal, or somewhere altogether more delicious, in Soho perhaps, where the ponces go?"

I did not know what a ponce was either, but the word had an instant effect on the colour of Dennis's complexion. He tried to speak, but David, whose expression was a mixture of exasperation and determination, wouldn't let him. "Don't demean yourself, Dennis," he said wearily. Then, unexpectedly, he turned to me. "Clara, my dear, allow me to apologize for Aidan's unpleasant behaviour. But his contract to complete this picture was drawn up by very competent lawyers, as was yours. I'm afraid that unless something quite untoward happens, you must see the adventures of Charles and Eloise out together till the very end."

I did not know how to answer. I stole a look at Aidan, who gave me a bemused smile, half-obscured by cigarette smoke. I decided the smile was insolent and did not return it. I had no wish to smile at him; in fact, I wished the lawyers had *not* been so competent. My life would be a great deal easier if I did not have to contend with Aidan every day! For him to be sacked, how much more "untoward" would his behaviour have to be than what we had witnessed tonight?

David raised his voice. "Very well, everyone," he announced wearily. "Thank you very much. Seven o'clock start tomorrow, as usual."

We dispersed. I submitted to Maria's undressing and re-dressing like a doll, my mind busy. I slathered cold cream over my face and neck and removed my make-up, then reapplied foundation, lipstick and eyeliner. I no longer ventured outside my hotel bedroom without what my mam would call my "slap". An actress had to look like an actress.

Maria handed me my hat and the fox fur I had bought with my first week's salary. Every society lady had a fox fur, though no one in Haverth had ever worn one, to my knowledge. Mine was very beautiful, the tail sleek and voluminous, the body cosy against my neck, the skull-less head expertly moulded to appear as it had in life. It had a tortoiseshell clip under its tail which, when I wound it round myself, fitted into the open mouth, securing the fur. When I put it on I always felt utterly grown-up, as far removed as possible from the young girl in the second-hand shoes who had waved to the camera on a newsreel only a few months ago.

Once my hat was pinned on and we had checked my stockings for ladders and my shoes for scuffs, Maria opened the dressing-room door for me to pass through. My car would be waiting. "Good evening, Miss Hope," she said.

I felt unsettled and inexplicably depressed. What if the animosity between Aidan and the rest of us were to appear on screen despite Aidan's acting skills? What if the money men didn't like the film, or it didn't get finished, and everything went wrong? My career as a film actress would be over without anyone even knowing my name. Mam and Da and Frank would be crushingly disappointed, And I would be heartbroken.

The car drew up and the driver opened the door for me. I got in but had barely settled myself when the door on the other side opened and David slid into the seat beside me. "Good God, Clara, I need a drink!" He leaned across me to speak to the driver. "Eddie, the Ritz!"

David took a cigarette from the silver case he always carried with him and felt in his pockets for matches. When he had lit the cigarette he drew on it with satisfaction, then slumped in the seat and let his head loll backwards. "Jesus, what a day! Aidan really is impossible." He glanced at me. "Oh, I'm so sorry" – he waved the cigarette case – "should I have offered you one?"

"No, thank you. I don't smoke."

He put the case in his pocket. "You will. Now, tell me truthfully. Are you happy?"

"Happy?" I was not sure what he meant. "Er ... yes, of course."

"Despite that ridiculous fellow?"

I hesitated. What did he wish me to say? That I would tolerate Aidan's behaviour for the sake of the actual takes, during which he outacted me, or that I would prefer a different leading man, or perhaps that I cared not a bit one way or another? Before I could speak, David rolled his head sideways and looked at me. "No, I should not have asked you that. You are too professional to criticize him to me."

I returned his look. My heart thudded a little, thrilled by the ease of his manner. It was delightful to be treated as the grown-up I was beginning to consider myself. I took in once again how handsome he was and felt my colour rise, though in the semi-darkness of the car he probably could not see it. "Do not say that, David," I told him. "I am not professional at all, you know. I have never had an acting lesson in my life." Now it had started, the confession I longed to make tumbled out. "I just muddle through, hoping I am doing the right thing and that I will not make too much of a fool of myself."

"Oh, stuff and nonsense!" David leaned forward and faced me, his knees touching mine. "Do you think I chose you merely because you are young and very beautiful and would look pretty on the screen?"

Very beautiful! My heart leapt to my throat. I could not speak. But David answered his own question. "Of course not! When I saw that newsreel, I had no idea that I would pick anyone out of it. I was not talent scouting — I was really only half watching it, to tell the truth — but that glimpse of you was enough. I telephoned to Bunniford that very moment." He began to act it, using his director's voice. " 'Get me that girl in the unflattering hat who appears about ninety seconds in!' I told him. 'I want her for my next picture!' " He moved even closer to me, and spoke in his ordinary voice. "The fact is, Clara, my dear, though you were on the screen for only one hundred and one frames, I went over those one hundred and one frames several times, and each time I grew more convinced you are an actress by nature. All the training in the world cannot better that, you know."

I had calmed a little, and could breathe. But I was mystified. "Frames?" I asked. "Like a frame round a painting, you mean?"

He laughed delightedly and puffed on his cigarette. As he exhaled, the smoke went up my nose and I coughed. "My dear child," said David, waving the cloud of smoke away, "has no one explained? Then allow me!"

He rested his cigarette on the ashtray so that he could use his hands to demonstrate. "A film is a long strip of pictures taken by the camera. You see the camera operator winding the reel of film through as he films, do you not?"

I nodded. David held up the palm of his left hand and made rolling movements over it with his right. "Well, when the film is shown, it is passed over a light at the correct speed, and the pictures seem to move." He picked up his cigarette and flicked the ash off the end. "Each second, twenty-four frames pass over the light, which is the speed that gives the most natural-looking movement we can achieve."

I considered this. "So the one hundred and one frames during which I was on the newsreel took ... about four seconds to show?"

"Roughly, yes. Good God, Eddie!" he admonished the driver, "are you driving a car or a *horse*? Faster, man!"

"Four seconds?" I was amazed. I counted four seconds to myself as I sat there, trying to digest the information that such a tiny space of time had transformed my existence. The newsreel had been filmed on May Day, the first of May. Now, as I looked out of the window at the hazy August sky and the thick foliage of the hedgerows, I was filled with disbelief. How could so much have happened so quickly? Less than four months ago I had been a farmer's daughter whose only connection with films was the Pier Pavilion Café – and my imagination. Now, I was travelling in a smart car with a fur around my neck, sitting beside a director. I felt like Cinderella on her way to the ball.

"Believe me, Clara, that four seconds was enough," said David. "You see, I had a strong suspicion that you would be good, and when I saw your screen test I knew I was right." He straightened up in the seat and looked absently out of the window, his chin resting on his hand. In profile, intermittently lit by the slanting sunlight, his good looks took on a different aspect; I could see the muscles in his cheeks and jaw, and note how perfectly formed his ears were, and how delicate the shape of his nose. He was without doubt the most beautiful man I had ever seen. Not for the first time, I wondered if he had ever tried his own hand at acting.

"I felt such an idiot," I told him. "I was sure I would get a letter saying 'thank you for attending, but we do not wish to see you again'."

"You did not *look* an idiot. You looked as I had predicted: graceful in movement and expression, and able to convey emotions. You know, because the audience cannot hear their words, I always look for actors and actresses who can act 'big', though not so big that it becomes over-theatrical."

The only theatrical productions I had seen were amateur ones in Aberaeron Church Hall, which had not impressed me much. "Like acting in the theatre, you mean?"

David pondered, still gazing out. The buildings had become taller and the traffic had increased; we were nearing the centre of London. "Like *some* acting in the theatre," he said. "I have seen wonderful, realistic acting on the stage, and I have seen execrable overacting too. In films, we have to strike a balance. And you are very good at it indeed." He turned away from the window and smiled, his thoughtful expression transforming into tenderness as I watched. "For which I shall be eternally grateful. Good actresses, who are as exquisitely formed as you in face and figure, are very difficult to find. Now, Eddie has at last got a move on. We shall be at the hotel in good time for cocktails." He squeezed my arm. "What will you have? A gin sling?"

When I described the Ritz Hotel to Mam and Da in my next letter home, I concentrated on the vastness and opulence of the building, the uniformed bell boys, the fashionable clothes I saw and the deliciousness of the dinner David and I ate there. I did not tell them that the gin sling David ordered for me tasted like medicine, so he drank it himself while I got through three much sweeter champagne cocktails before we even sat down at the table and half a bottle of wine while I was eating. Neither did I mention that as the evening went on, the crowd around us became louder and more abandoned, the waiters busier, the music faster and the atmosphere increasingly like an enormous party.

It was as if everyone there was celebrating something, though it was not a special occasion. I saw gentlemen lay ten-shilling and even pound notes down on the tables without so much as blinking. I saw ladies with silk stockings, feathered headbands and permanently waved hair smoking cigarettes in ebony holders. I saw laughing and chattering and, later on, hand-holding and kissing across tables. But most important, I was with a charming man, who, I realized with heart-stopping excitement, was himself charmed. By *me*.

It was the most enjoyable evening I had ever experienced. David was at ease with the wealth surrounding him. He was known to the hotel staff and exchanged pleasantries with them and with several groups of people who greeted him as we passed. Most delightful of all, every woman who entered the dining room noticed David. Some allowed their gaze to alight on him after a few seconds, some only after they were seated and had begun to look around. They whispered to their escorts, who would then turn as unobtrusively as they could and look at David too. He took no notice, but I allowed my imagination to race away. What must they be saying? *"Look, there is David Penn, the film director. And who is that lovely girl with him? What an exquisite fur she's wearing!"*

Looking back, such speculation was childish, but I was not so much a child as to betray any confidences to my parents. I told them nothing, though all I could think of as

I wrote was the delicious knowledge that David had singled me out and taken me to the smartest hotel in London. When he had opened the car door for me to go home alone because he had decided to stay at his club for the night, he had put his hands on my shoulders and kissed my cheek softly, his lips barely brushing my skin. "Good night, princess," he had said. "Thank you for a wonderful evening. Sleep well, and I'll see you at seven o'clock."

Dazed and happy, I had climbed into the car. And before he closed the door, he had leaned in and kissed me again, with a little more purpose.

Of course, the next morning I felt ill. I staggered downstairs and into the car, and at the studio Maria looked at me, smiled and brought me a glass of water. I drank it, and several more, and took with gratitude the aspirins she offered. "I must be sickening for something," I told her apologetically. "I hope I don't start sneezing in the middle of a scene."

She was still smiling. "You won't."

Luckily, David wanted to film other people's scenes first that day. I lay on the sofa in my dressing room, waiting to feel better. In the middle of the morning, there was a knock on the door.

Assuming it was David, I sat up eagerly. "Come in!"

It was Aidan. He was in costume, without his wig, as usual, and looking untidy; it took me a few seconds to realize that he had not yet shaved that day, and the make-up people had not started on him. "Your dressing room's bigger than mine," he said mildly. "I suppose that means you're the star of this fiasco. So, I hear you and David hit the town last night."

"Well, we went to the Ritz," I told him blankly. Keeping my voice unenthusiastic would, I hoped, encourage him to go away.

"Judging by the look of you, you must have put away a fair amount." He smiled, not very sincerely. "More than David, I'd say."

I neither remembered nor cared how much David had drunk. I did not reply but closed my eyes and lay back on my cushions. I heard nothing for a couple of minutes. Then, assuming Aidan had gone, I opened my eyes. He was sitting on my dressing stool, his elbows on his knees, his hands hanging loosely. On his face was a look of such ... intensity, I can only call it, that I actually flinched.

"What are you afraid of?" he asked.

73

His tone was not his usual light, careless one, nor was it his "acting" one. There was something in it I had not heard before. And he went on looking at me, his eyes full of questions.

"I do not know what you mean," I said truthfully.

"Just then, when you saw me. You started, as if afraid. Why?"

"I was surprised. I thought you had gone."

"Is that all?"

"Of course." I swung my feet down to the floor and faced him squarely. "Aidan, I do not feel well, and I do not wish to answer these pointless questions. Will you please let me alone? I will see you later in the studio."

Suddenly his hands shot out and grasped both mine. "Clara, you must take care. Promise me you will take care?"

I tried to pull away, but he held my hands very tightly. "Let go!" I protested.

He did not loosen his grip. Understanding that he wouldn't do so until I answered him, I sighed and spoke patiently, as if to a child. "Look, Aidan. What could I need to 'take care' about? Nothing the slightest" – what was that word David had used about Aidan's behaviour? – "untoward has happened."

"Very well." Dropping my hands, he took hold of a pen I had left on the dressing table and fumbled under Comte de Montfort's embroidered jacket until he found a small piece of paper. He smoothed it out; it was a cigarette paper. "Please, Clara, take this."

I waited, irritated, while he wrote something on the paper. "And be aware, too," he went on, "that some people care about you a great deal and will be there if you ever need their help. Do not disregard them." He looked at me sadly, holding out the cigarette paper. "And do not disregard yourself."

That night I dreamt I was in Haverth. But a dream-village had been substituted for the Haverth I knew. The church and the school and the pub were in their usual places, but surrounding them were hordes of people. They were silent, as people in dreams often are, but it was clear they were angry. My gaze travelled over the crowd like a camera. Many people looked back at me; some turned their heads away. Each of them – hundreds and hundreds – carried an unmistakable air of disapproval.

I was standing on the steps of the school, where Mr

Reynolds always stood when he rang the bell in the mornings. Haverth School's register was a formality; the headmaster made a point of greeting every child by name as they entered and bidding them goodbye at the end of the day. But in my dream there were no schoolchildren, just this hostile crowd pressing towards me from all sides. And, I realized in horror, I was standing there in my petticoat. I tried to cover my body with my hands, but other hands came from nowhere and tore mine away, determinedly exposing me.

Everyone was staring. They began to point and whisper and jeer, and although they were as silent as if they were in a film, I knew what they were saying. *Act-ress, act-ress, act-ress*, they chanted. *Furs* and *pearls* and *champagne*! One woman, a stranger like the others, put her face close to mine and whispered, *Do you think you are impressing us, Clara Hope? You're just a country girl, as ignorant as a cow in your da's field, and we all know it!*

I clutched the sheet around me. Light was flooding my bedroom; I surfaced from the depths of sleep. I lay there with my eyes still closed, confused and uncomfortably hot, and with a pain I can only describe as heartache in my breast.

I opened my eyes and stretched my stiff limbs. The hotel room was as I had left it the night before – thickly carpeted, with a high ceiling and tall windows, as unlike any house within twenty miles of Haverth as it was possible to be. Sighing, I pushed back the covers. The people in my dream had frightened me. But however much my heart ached for all that was familiar, I had come too far to retreat. The cinema audience, who would pay for their ticket and expect to be entertained, were the ones who would pass judgement upon me.

"Marjorie!" exclaimed David. "My dear, how *delicious* to see you! How was New York?"

"Oh … you know – American," said the woman Jeanette had just ushered into the studio. She was young, very slim, very well groomed and very expensively dressed. Her hair was the shiniest blonde I had ever seen – unnaturally so, like a gold skull cap – and her face was as delicately painted as a doll's. "And hot, so hot!" She sat down in David's director's chair and gave him a conspiratorial smile. "I am not interrupting anything *vital*, am I?"

"Not at all." David swept his arm around the room in a theatrical gesture. "All right, everyone, we're finished for today. *Au revoir*, till seven tomorrow!"

I was intrigued by the sudden appearance of this woman and by the effect she had on David.

He did not usually say things like "delicious" and *"au revoir"*, or allow anyone to sit in his chair, or pretend visitors were not interrupting. His normal reaction was to shout at them to get out, and what did they think this was, Piccadilly Circus?

No filming had been in progress when she arrived or she would not have been allowed into the studio. We had been preparing for tomorrow's work. David had been discussing the scene we were to do first thing the following morning, which would include a fight between Aidan and two men called "stuntmen". They were playing ruffians who set upon the Comte in a back street. I had to show horror, hit one of them with the pistol Aidan had dropped, and, when the villains had run off, sink to my knees "gracefully, Clara, not like a sack of potatoes!" and go to his aid as he lay on the floor.

It would need quite a few takes. We would do it several times, then the best would be edited together afterwards. It was always very tedious waiting about in full costume under hot lights while David decided whether or not to do another take. Maria was forever powdering my face, as perspiration was only allowed to appear on screen when demanded for the drama. And if David wasn't quite satisfied, we would have to set the whole scene up another day and do it yet again.

People began to leave. I noticed Jeanette give David a look as she pushed the studio doors, but I did not understand its meaning. Aidan nodded carelessly to Marjorie but did not speak to her. Instead, he turned to me. "Well, David seems occupied this evening. Shall you and I have dinner together?"

I could not think of an excuse quickly enough, so I found myself sitting opposite Aidan in the almost deserted dining room of my hotel. I pushed pieces of chicken around my plate while Aidan lounged in his chair, smoking, his other hand around a tumbler of whisky, his dinner cooling on the table.

It was not like being with David. I did not feel elated or even tipsy, though I had ordered wine in the hope that alcohol would anaesthetise me. I felt disappointed that David had ignored me and curious about the woman, and resentful of Aidan's ability to needle me. Eventually, as Aidan at last picked up his knife and fork, I could no longer restrain myself. "So who is she?"

"Who?"

"You know perfectly well."

He put his head on one side and considered his Dover sole and potatoes. "Jealous?"

"Why on earth would I be jealous?" I replied steadily. "I am merely asking for information, since no one introduced her to me."

"Her name is Marjorie Cunningham."

"I did not ask her name. I asked who she is."

"She is Marjorie Cunningham."

"Aidan!"

I had spoken louder than I intended. A waiter looked up from folding napkins in the corner, gave me a sour look and resumed his work. "Aidan," I hissed. "You know what I mean, so please stop being so tiresome. Is she … well, is she David's…"

"Lover?"

"I was going to say 'lady friend'."

He grinned. "How quaint!"

I strove for patience. "Can you not just give me the information without this performance?"

Setting down his cutlery, he sipped his drink and look at me with amusement. "Very well. She is an actress, like you." He put down his glass and held it between his hands, his gaze still on my face. "Though not very like you, actually. She is unscrupulous, vain and grasping." He mused for a moment. "But striking, I'm sure you will agree."

I did not consider Marjorie Cunningham particularly striking. I had seen only a fashionably willowy frame, artificially gilded hair and a pricey fur. "Men's appreciation of what is striking must be different from women's," I said. I put some chicken in my mouth and chewed while Aidan watched me, the amused look still in his eyes. "She is certainly *glamorous*," I added, "but that is not the same thing."

Aidan turned his attention once more to his plate. I noticed that his hair had too much oil in it and that he had not removed all of his make-up: a pale line of it ran round his hairline and chin like the beach at the edge of the land. For an actor, he took little care of his appearance. "She is one of David's set. They are always at his parties, drinking and dancing and making fools of themselves. You know he has a house on an island in the river, not far from here?"

I did not know this. And to my knowledge, David had not given any parties since I had been working on the film. If he had, I had not been invited. My heartbeat stuttered.

"Marjorie's been in America trying to get a part in a picture," continued Aidan. "I think she has been in a play on Broadway or something. In any case, she must have failed to get into 'the movies', as they call them there, or she would not be back here in Old England."

An unwelcome thought came to me. "Do you think she is hoping for a part in our film?"

He laughed loudly. The waiter looked round again. "*Our*

film? Oh, Clara, you are sweet! Marjorie has not come to David for a *part*! And this film is not ours at all. It belongs to that band of scroungers David is in thrall to. His so-called backers. A worse pack of villains you could not wish to find. Now eat up your food like a good girl and let's not talk about Marjorie any more."

We did not mention Marjorie again, but she remained in my thoughts. When the waiter offered pudding and coffee I refused, thanked Aidan for dinner and bade him good night. He stood politely when I rose from the table. As I left the dining room I could feel him looking at me. Once in my room I threw my fur onto the bed, took off my hat and studied my reflection.

Striking. What did Aidan mean by the word? And when he used it to describe Marjorie, did he mean that I was *not* striking? I had called her glamorous, which I was sure I was not. So what *was* I?

David had said I was beautiful, though neither Aidan nor

I had used this word to describe Marjorie. Was being beautiful different from being striking or glamorous? Marjorie and I were both young women – I estimated her age at twenty-three or -four – who took care of our appearance. We had both abandoned the long hair of our childhood for the "bob", though Marjorie's was a sleeker, shorter cut than mine and heavily bleached. I turned my head from side to side. Did *glamour* lie in bleached hair? She and I both wore cosmetics on our faces, though I had not gone as far as to pluck my eyebrows and paint them on in a more fashionable position, as I had noticed she had done. Did that make her *striking*?

I leaned on the dressing-table, cupping my chin in my hands. My hair could perhaps do with a tidy-up: as it was curlier than Marjorie's and more liable to unruliness. But I could not see any further improvement I could make to my appearance. I could not change the colour of my eyes or the darkness of my lashes and brows, or the shape of my lips. My nose, which I now considered more carefully than I had ever done before, was exactly like Mam's: short and unobtrusive, with small nostrils. It looked all right on her. Did it look all right on me? And would it look all right on a big screen, high above the audience's heads?

Exposure, ridicule, censure. I looked away from the mirror.

All actresses must feel like this, I reasoned. Marjorie Cunningham must feel like this. Even Lilian Hall-Davis must feel like this. I put my hand over my heart, feeling it beating under my breast. The thought of Marjorie's heart beating under *her* breast made me feel uncertain. She might be striking and glamorous, and maybe even beautiful, but she did not seem *real*. She was like something inanimate, designed by another hand.

David's, perhaps?

I stole another glance at my reflection. My face was its usual pale self, but there was resolve in its expression. I would not allow David to prefer Marjorie, or any other woman, to me. *Ignore her,* I told myself. *Show David that you scarcely noticed that he left with her without even introducing us.*

I would not be so childish as to have a moment's anxiety. David had taken *me* to the Ritz; he had kissed *me* beside the car; he had told *me* I was beautiful. In his company I felt grown-up, alive and sophisticated. Aidan, who made me feel like the eighteen-year-old I was, was just jealous. He had asked me to dinner because he was trying to get me to become his ... I hesitated even to think of the word he had used about Marjorie and David ... *lover.* It was not a word used at home. There, you could be a man's "lady friend" or, less approvingly, his "fancy woman". "Lover" conjured up connotations of illicit affairs. But David was the only man I wanted to be my "gentleman friend". And surely – even in Aidan's cynical estimation – beautiful trumped striking and glamorous every time.

The filming went on. When it was sunny, scenes were done outside on one of the "stages", as they were called, though they were not stages at all. They were huge areas of empty ground pretending to be somewhere in France. Sometimes it would be a hayfield, for which hay was brought from somewhere, and sometimes a Paris square, with tricolours draped on the flimsy balconies and wooden cobbles underfoot. One of the stages even pretended to be the English Channel, with an enormous pool of water over which was rigged up the front part of an eighteenth-century sailing ship. A wind machine blew the sail, but it also blew my hair across my face, prompting an infuriated "Get it right or get off my picture, you fool!" from David in the direction of poor Alfie and the need to redo the whole scene.

During those days, everyone spoke to me except the one person whose company I desired. My mood veered from desperation when David turned away from me to excitement when he looked at me, from isolation within my own bleak thoughts to loud conversation and laughter in a group of people vying for my attention, all trying to outdo one another to entertain me. I was the star, the centre of attention; I was someone new, someone ignorant of film-making; someone they could impress.

Simona Vincenza, however, resented me. She was only a little older than I was, and her Italian professional name disguised an Irishwoman from Liverpool, but the airs she gave herself were astonishing. My friends back in Haverth would have been merciless. One evening, Godfrey, the Scot, took everyone out to a nightclub in London to celebrate his birthday, and Simona and I found ourselves in the same car.

"So you're from Wales, I understand?" she said in her languid way. Everything about her was slow: the way she dipped and raised her head or her eyelids; the way she spoke; the way she drifted about the studios, trailing a wrap or a fur coat if she considered it too cold, though it was only September.

"Yes, from a place called Haverth."

Her look was questioning.

"Near Aberaeron."

Her eyes closed and opened again, slowly. They remained questioning.

"Which is quite near Aberystwyth."

"All these Abers!" She began to smile a little. She always lipsticked a bow shape onto her real lips, and when she smiled her mouth looked to me like the fleshy open mouth of a chimpanzee.

"I wonder you don't get mixed up!"

"Oh, we manage."

"And what does your father do?"

I was tempted to ask her why she could possibly wish to know this, but prudence stopped me. This woman and I had to work together for the foreseeable future. If she could not be civil to me, I must at all costs remain civil to her. "He is a farmer," I said. "We have cows, and we also grow grain and vegetables."

The chimpanzee smile widened. "Leeks, I suppose?"

I did not grace this with an answer but turned to look out of the car window. After a short silence, Simona began again. "My ancestors were farmers too, in Ireland. Though of course that was long ago. My grandfather sailed to England and became a very successful businessman, and my father runs the business now."

"Fancy," was all I said. I had no wish to play her game of "my family's better than yours, so why are you the star and not me?". She could resent me all she wished, it would not reverse our roles. Jealousy, I had learned by now, was as great a part of an actor's existence as learning lines or having their face powdered. And how delicious it felt to be the object of it, instead of the victim!

At the end of that uneasy drive with Simona I found myself in the intoxicated company of my fellow actors in a dark, smoky cellar full of noisy people and moody waiters. I ate and drank little; I had no appetite for food, alcohol or company. The thoughts in my head were alien from them, and from the place, as if my surroundings moved in a dream around the real, conscious me. I did not want champagne and dancing; I wanted only David, who was not there.

Where was he tonight? He had not spoken to me except as director and actress for weeks. Had he avoided Godfrey's birthday party because he knew I would be here? Was he now regretting having been so nice to me that night? Was he at his house on the island? Was Marjorie there too, or had she gone back to New York?

I looked around me. Aidan, who was seated at the other end of the table, ignored me. Robert was at his elbow, and Godfrey at mine, while Simona, opposite Aidan, made eyes at him, which he also ignored. The woman who played

Simona's maid no longer appeared on the call list; she must have finished her scenes with Simona and gone. Having no scenes of my own with her, I had never even met her.

Toying with my glass, I pondered on the haphazard nature of filming. There was something called a "shooting schedule", but it was often disrupted by someone not appearing punctually or David changing his mind about what he wanted to do that day. Scenes were done again several times or filmed in sections, days or weeks apart. Kitty's job of photographing the film set and the actors at the end of every scene was vital. Each evening David looked at the "rushes", the bits of filming done that day. Each morning he wanted something done again.

I found it baffling. The beheading scene had been filmed in the second week because the sun was out. As Eloise, I naturally would be in despair at Charles de Montfort's death. But this scene had not been filmed yet, all these weeks later. It would probably be done indoors in the studio, with artificial light shining on me instead of the sun, and I would have nothing to show my despair to but the unblinking eye of the camera. The close-ups would be filmed separately, after a long session in the make-up room. Then the bits of film from the outdoor guillotining scene would be "spliced", as they called it, onto the bits of film of me despairing, and the audience would think it was all happening at the same time. A film, I reflected despondently, was all lies.

Fairyland indeed. And full of witches, like any children's story.

I sighed. Perhaps a little too loudly, because Godfrey turned his head, concerned. "Are you well, Clara dear?"

"Yes, perfectly, thank you." I tried to brighten my expression. "I was just ... Godfrey, don't you ever think that the way we do a film, cutting it in bits, then sticking them together, is just ... lying?"

His elegant features disappeared under a beaming smile. "Oh, Clara, you are wonderful! It is not lying, it is *illusion*, which is the essence of entertainment! Audiences don't care if what they see is authentic. They only want to be moved, to tears or laughter or both. So that's what we do for them: we give them what they want. And it's not cutting up and sticking together, it's called *editing*. Here, let me pour you some more bubbly. Good for a weary soul, don't y'know."

I put my hand over my glass. "No, thank you, Godfrey. And my soul is not weary, but I'm afraid my body is. Would you be so good as to call me a taxi? I simply must go back and get some sleep."

This speech was worthy of Jeanette or Simona or even, I supposed, Marjorie. It came out in a high, clipped tone I did not recognize as my own voice. Yet when I was with these people I could not help copying their speech. David's "stuff and nonsense!" and Godfrey's frequent unquestioning question, "don't y'know", would never find their way into the mouths of anyone at home, yet they seemed natural to me now.

I was half proud and half ashamed. I longed to be accepted by these people, yet I did not feel comfortable in their world. I admired and despised them simultaneously. Even my infatuation with David did not smother the knowledge that his behaviour was erratic and sometimes unfathomable. And yet I wanted him desperately, as desperately as I wanted to be in, and yet not of, this topsy-turvy out-of-sequence world.

"Oh, come on, Clara," called Robert, who had overheard my request. "This place serves after hours. It's got good strong doors and an excellent warning system, so don't worry about the police and their silly licensing laws." He raised his glass. "We'll be here till dawn and go straight to Sheppers in the morning!"

I used my new voice again, giggling apologetically. "But I need my beauty sleep!" I trilled, leaving unsaid the reason, but knowing it was implied: *after all, I am the star!*

Aidan shot me an amused look, the first look of any kind he had given me that evening. "Better do as the lady wishes, Godfrey. When Miss Hope speaks, we obey."

Godfrey whispered something to a waiter, and we said our goodbyes, kissing cheeks as was the fashion in Paris, and therefore in London. Robert and Godfrey expressed their regret that I was leaving so early, but Simona said nothing. I was glad she was jealous of me. And if Aidan was truly what she wanted, she was welcome to him.

As soon as I got back to the hotel I went to my room and slammed the door. And then, I am ashamed to admit, I sprawled on the bed and cried. I had been so certain that David liked me. I had even persuaded myself that he would fall in love with me and that we would be married and live on the French Riviera, or wherever film stars lived. But his attentions to me might as well not have happened. It was as if we had acted a scene, and now that it was over he had forgotten all about it.

He was interested in people like Marjorie Cunningham and the jewelled women who had greeted him at the Ritz, who hovered around the actors who hovered around me. But I did not care about any of these people with their shiny cars and cigarette holders and slicked-down hair, who looked like puppets when they danced that stupid dance that involved putting your knees together and kicking up your legs. I only cared about David. *He* would not make a fool of himself doing that dance, I was sure. He was sensible, grown-up and clever, and so beautiful that my heart raced whenever I looked at him.

These thoughts brought on a new bout of tears. When I had recovered a little I went to the basin in the corner of my room, washed my face and gave my reflection a stern talking to. *Of course he likes sophisticated women. He knows tons of people. He's a well-known film director. He has a house on an island and is a member of a London gentlemen's club. He is so much older and wiser and more desirable than you, Sarah Freebody. However can you think he might love you?*

But lecturing myself did not stop my love. Love is beyond logic; it is a kind of lunacy that rationality cannot penetrate. David had shown me attention, but he had given no sign of being in love with me. That was no barrier to my longing, though. I yearned for more nights like the one at the Ritz, when he had been so attentive and called me "princess". And such fervent longing is so deeply painful, it is as close to madness as love itself.

I dreaded the darkness. Summer was fading; leaves were thick on the lawns in the hotel grounds and on the roadsides. Tomorrow morning I would rise before dawn, and tomorrow evening I would return in a different, dusky September darkness. But every day, I lived in a darkness of my own making, at the bottom of a deep well of impossible, irrepressible love.

"Clara, dearest, are you free this evening?"

It was a murmur, close to my ear as I stood in the area behind the camera, watching Aidan and Robert do the same scene they had done five times already. But it was a moment of revelation, as if the studio lights had been switched on and shone with sudden, blinding brilliance. I stiffened with anticipation. David was so close to me I could smell the cigarette smoke and perspiration in his shirt. "Yes," I whispered.

"It seems so long since I've managed to get any time with you," he said, still keeping his voice low. "But you are my best girl, you know. Did you miss me?"

"Very much."

I did not ask why he had ignored me until now, when the film was almost finished. I did not ask why he had not come out in the evenings with me and the others. I did not ask where he went when each day's work was done. The moment he spoke, it had ceased to matter. A girl in love is gloriously selfish, thinking only of the strength of her own feelings and anxious for a sign of his. He gave it in the form of a squeeze of my hand and a flash of a smile. "Shall I come to the hotel? You are not going out to dinner, are you?"

"No, I am quite free."

"Then let us order dinner in a private room so that we can be together with no distractions." He looked at me with the almost amused look I knew well. "You do not object to spending the evening alone with me?"

My heart swooped. "No, of course not."

"I assure you, I am a gentleman."

"I know that, David."

"Then I will arrange it all. Shall you meet me in the foyer at eight o'clock?"

I nodded and stood there trembling as David turned calmly back to the rehearsal. "All right, everybody, let's try a take. Maria, where are you? Aidan's nose is shining like a lighthouse. Bernard, get the board."

While Maria was powdering his face, I sensed, more than actually saw, Aidan's eyes slide in my direction. He had probably noticed my whispered conversation with

David. Well, I thought carelessly, if he wished to spend his time being jealous, then he was at liberty to do that. The notion made me smile. Having made Simona jealous of me and Aidan jealous of David, why should I not be amused? The entire thing was folly of the first order.

David had ordered champagne cocktails. "You like these, don't you?" he asked, raising his glass and smiling at me across the table in a charming first-floor room the hotel hired out for private parties. It had swagged curtains and a view of the river. I realized it must be above the main dining room, where I had eaten that uncomfortable meal with Aidan.

"I *love* champagne cocktails!" I raised my glass too, watching the sugar lump at the bottom sending its spray of bubbles towards the surface. "They are so pretty!" I took a sip. "And sweet, too!"

"Are you speaking of the drink or of yourself?" asked David archly.

Thrilled by this gallantry, I laughed. "I do not consider

myself pretty, or sweet. But if you care to think I am, that is your business."

"Then I will cherish that belief." He drank some of his cocktail. "As I cherish your company, my dear."

I drank too, and we grinned at each other. I had never known such happiness. I was full of an energy and restlessness I could not explain. I felt as if I could spread my arms wide and fly out of the window on a cushion of pure contentment. David – my darling, beautiful David – was here with me instead of somewhere else, with someone else. My feelings had no boundaries; the certainty that *I did not love in vain* filled the universe. "And I yours," I told him.

As we began our meal, which I scarcely ate, David explained why he had been so busy. "I had things to deal with at the house," he said, "you know, this place I've recently bought. It needs renovating and modernizing. The bathrooms are a nightmare. I'm living there, but it's not fit for visitors."

I dismissed the memory of Aidan telling me that David held parties there. Jealousy again. Aidan lived in a flat in London. I did not know what it was like, but it could not possibly be as smart as a house on an island with, apparently, more than one bathroom. The houses in Haverth, I reflected uncharitably, had no bathrooms at all.

"So now, thankfully," David was saying, "those infernal architects and insurers and heaven knows what have left me alone, at least temporarily, and I can devote this evening to my favourite pastime: having dinner with a beautiful girl." He twinkled at me, sipping wine. "Now that the filming is almost done, and I shall be shut up in that stuffy editing room with those tedious men and their little machines for God knows how long, I must get my fill of my dear Clara while I can, must I not?"

I smiled shyly. I never knew how to behave when he said such things. "Um … so how much longer will filming last, do you think?"

"Well, the money men are satisfied with progress so far, and I *think* I'm satisfied with what we've already done. There'll be a break over Christmas and New Year, of course, but we're scheduled to finish at the end of January, and provided nothing goes drastically wrong, I think we will."

Christmas was two weeks away. January was thirty-one days long. I had only about six weeks before my reason to be with David would disappear. Unless, of course, there was a different, more permanent reason for us to be together. "What will you do next?" I asked conversationally. "Another film for David Penn Productions?"

He considered for a moment, his eyes on my face. "Actually, Clara my dear, I am thinking of following in Marjorie's footsteps and trying my hand in California. Of course, I have a better chance of success than she ever did. She is quite deluded, you know."

I was dismayed. "America! But you are a success *here*!"

"Exactly." He leaned forward eagerly. "So I can be a

greater success *there*. California is where the future of film-making is. They have a lot of space, fine weather and people who are prepared to put money into the industry and make it into something really big. I have some contacts there who are keen to introduce me to the men who matter. I really feel I should take the opportunity."

Seeing my disappointment, he took my hand. "We'll have to see how this film does," he said gently, "but I'm willing to wager that there will be plenty of other opportunities for Clara Hope, here and in California. If she wishes to seize them, of course."

Did he mean he might take me with him? I could not ask. "Clara Hope is ready for anything!" I blurted.

He laughed. "In that case, I am very glad to be in her company." He took the bottle of wine out of the cooler and filled my glass. "Drink up, my dear."

After dinner, the waiter set down a tray of coffee on a low table by the fireplace and left the room, closing the door noiselessly behind him. David sat on a small sofa and patted the cushion next to him. "Let us enjoy ourselves for a moment, shall we?"

I did not need such an invitation. As he spoke, I was already plumping myself down like a schoolgirl. My head felt light; my spirits were high. "Enjoy ourselves?" I repeated coquettishly. I felt as if I were acting in one of the scenes where I had to tempt Charles de Montfort with Eloise's feminine charm. I saw other girls flirt all the time, but I was not sure if David would consider it unbecoming.

It seemed not. He grinned charmingly. His hand went to his jacket pocket and he drew out an embossed box, unmistakably a jeweller's box. "But first, my dear," he said, "I implore you to accept this as a token of my regard."

My ears buzzed with wild thoughts: *It will not be a ring. It cannot not be a ring. If it is a ring, what will I say?* Breathless, I opened the box.

It was not a ring. It was a slim gold bracelet studded with green stones. When I looked at David his grin had become a half-doubtful smile, and in his eyes was the message, "please like my gift; I can't bear it if you reject me!"

"Oh, David, it's beautiful! I absolutely adore it. Thank you so much!" I took it from the box and held it up. In the artificial light, it glowed like fire. "Are these emeralds?"

His face clouded, though at the time I did not realize it was because of my lack of taste. "Of course," he said gently. "Nothing but the most beautiful jewels for the most beautiful lady. Consider it your Christmas present, a little early." He took it from my hand. "Here, let me put it on for you."

When he had done so, I held my wrist up, watching the green stones twinkle in the light. "I've never had such a glorious thing before, you know… I am so lucky, I can't—"

But I did not say the remainder of my sentence, because David's hands were suddenly drawing my face towards his and his lips descended on mine. It was a longer, more insistent kiss than the ones he had given me outside the Ritz. I did not know how to respond. No one had ever kissed me like this before. Boys in Haverth plonked their mouths in roughly the right place and fumbled drunkenly with blouse buttons and petticoats, but girls just pushed them away and laughed. No one had ever spoken to me with interested courtesy, complimented me and spent money on me. No one had ever been as worldly, rich and good-looking as David either. And no one had ever placed his lips – soft, searching, electrifying – so tenderly on mine.

I felt my body stiffen, but as he put his hands on the tops of my legs, and began to caress them gently, my muscles softened and we leaned against each other, chest to chest, lips to lips, absorbed in a world of sensation. The feeling was like electricity passing through me. My heart responded to the current that crackled around it, increasing its rate and changing its rhythm. I had never listened to my heart before, or felt its movements so keenly. But David's kiss made all the fibres and vessels and cells in my body suddenly more sensitive. Every bit of me leapt towards him, eager for more of the electric spark.

We went on kissing. I put my hands inside his jacket and held him tightly around his waist. He was a slim man, tall, though not very muscular. Under his shirt his flesh felt soft, yet not soft like my own flesh. I had never considered before what it was that made men so different from women, apart from the obvious things. But his flat, tubular body seemed the very height of masculinity. Touching him, I was aware that his hands – again, hands with fingers and thumbs like mine, yet *not* like mine – were touching me and giving him the same sensations as I was feeling. It was mutual attraction, and mutual desire. David and I were in love.

CAMERA

Sometimes we had snow in the village at Christmas, but that year was mild. Dampness hung in the air, showing misty over the mountains and clinging to hair and hats and overcoats. Haverth did not look picturesque. It looked, after my six-month absence, primitive. And *small*. How quickly I had become accustomed to my spacious hotel room! The privy at the bottom of the garden seemed insanitary, even though Mam scrubbed it every day. The garden itself, with its rows of cabbages and potatoes, lacked any beauty. And indoors the rooms seemed impossibly cramped, as if we were all trying to fit ourselves into a dolls' house.

Da kept saying, "I can't believe it's our Sarah!", and staring at me with moist eyes. When I arrived on Christmas Eve in the taxi from Aberaeron, Mam hugged me so tightly I had to fight her off so that I could breathe. And even Frank, whose new moustache made him look unrecognizably grown up, and far too conscious of himself to show his feelings, squeezed my shoulder. I wanted to embrace him, but had to content myself with admiring the facial hair and seeing his joy when I gave him the Christmas gift I'd brought.

"It's cells," I told him as he drew the wooden frame out of its box.

"I know what it is!"

"Well, Mam and Da might not."

Mam laughed. "Do you know what cells are, John?"

"It's that thing!" replied Da.

Frank was speechless. He put the framed film cells on the table and contemplated them in awe. Da inspected them too. "I still don't know what I'm looking at, love," he said to me.

"It's the film Sarah's in, see, Da." Frank had found his voice, which shook a little. "It's some of the bits that are all joined together to make the film, isn't it, Sair?"

I nodded. "I got sixteen because that's how many make one foot of film."

Mam was looking baffled. "One foot?"

"Unbelievable, isn't it?" I went on, feeling important. "A film is one long strip of these cells, or frames, they sometimes call them, and when the strip is passed over the light, the pictures appear to move." I could not resist adding the particle of knowledge I had cherished ever since David had imparted it to me. "Do you know, for every second of film, twenty-four of these little bits go in front of the light? One hundred make just over four seconds of film."

Frank had gone pink with pleasure. "People like me *never* get hold of them!"

"People like film stars' brothers, you mean?" teased Mam. She poked Frank's shoulder. "What do you say to your sister now, Frank?"

"Oh, thank you, Sair!" He was too shy to kiss this new Sarah, who wore a layer of paint on her face and expensive scent behind her ears. But he picked up my gift and held it to his chest as tenderly as any lover. "I'll treasure it." Suddenly, something occurred to him. "How did you get them? I bet you stole them!"

"She did *not* steal them!" Mam was indignant, though Da was laughing. "Frank Freebody, you take that back!"

I was glad of Mam's intervention. It gave me time to compose myself for the moment I had been anticipating ever since I arrived. "I didn't steal them. I was given them by David Penn, the director of the film. If you hold them up to the light, Frank, you'll see that I'm in them. Less than one second of me, but me nevertheless."

There. I'd said his name. And I didn't *think* I'd gone red or fidgeted while I said it.

But Mam was regarding me curiously. "You and this David Penn, then, are you … you know, stepping out?"

Stepping out. I tried not to cringe. That was a less approving version of "walking out", which was the Haverth term for courting with a possible view to marriage.

"No, of course not," I told her. And now I *did* go red. The blush crept up my neck and burned my cheeks. "He's the director of the film, that's all, and I told him my brother

107

liked films, and he said some cells from the film would be a nice Christmas present."

They were all looking at me. "And he was right, wasn't he?" I added brightly.

Florence and Mary wanted to hear every last detail about the film, the costumes, the hotel I was living in, the restaurants and nightclubs, the cars I had ridden in. They wanted to hear everything I could tell them about London. Florence, who had flung my fox fur around her neck the moment I took it off, demanded an exact description of the West End shop that had sold it to me. Mary asked me if the trains really went under the ground, or was that only in the pictures? They were so excited that they kept interrupting each other, their words tumbling out in a torrent. But both of them sat silent, their attention riveted, when I told them about David.

"So you're walking out with the *director*?" asked Mary incredulously. "I bet they're all jealous, aren't they?"

"Not exactly, no." Satisfying though her interest was, I

did not wish to exaggerate. "David does not wish to have it discussed. He can't stand gossip, he says, so I'm not sure how much the others know about—"

"Has he kissed you?" interrupted Mary.

"Oh, yes."

"Properly, she means," added Florence.

I couldn't help smiling. In the world of Haverth girls, "properly" meant "improperly". "Oh, yes," I said again. "And he's taken me to dinner loads of times, and he bought me this." I drew back my cuff and showed them the gold and emerald bracelet. "It's my Christmas present, a little early, he said."

Mary was enchanted, but Florence hardened her features and studied me. "How old is he?"

"I'm not sure. Twenty-five or twenty six?"

"So he's very successful, then. For his age, I mean. Must have rich parents."

"Perhaps." The idea that David might have parents, rich or otherwise, had never entered my consciousness. He never spoke of them, and since his whole demeanour was that of an entirely adult man, at ease in society, I had never thought to question how he had achieved this. "And he's clever," I added. "And makes films that people like. So investors give him money to make more films, and the films make money for him, and that's how it works."

"I see," said Flo. "So how did he get into this pictures business in the first place?"

"I don't know, Flo," I told her truthfully. "We've hardly

109

had time to discover every little thing about each other's lives, you know."

"I bet you haven't," she said airily. "Too busy doing something else! You know what people say about actresses, don't you?"

"Flo!" scolded Mary. Her colour rising, she turned to me in concern. "Don't listen to her, Sarah. She's only jealous. Actresses these days are nothing like … you know."

I sighed. "It's all right. Flo doesn't mean I'm the nearest thing to a prostitute, she means that people with old-fashioned ideas might *think* I am. Right, Flo?"

Florence did not reply.

"And anyway," I continued, "David's not like that at all. He's the loveliest man you could ever hope to meet, and I'm the luckiest girl in the world because he cares for me."

"Let's hope he does," said Florence. She took off my fur and handed it back, her face inscrutable. "It's obvious you care for him. But you know, Sair, when Bobby Pritchard went out with Glenys Harding behind my back, when I was sure he was my true love, my mam said to me, 'The heart can be mistaken.'"

My heart was not mistaken. When I returned to the hotel after Christmas, I had not taken three steps across the foyer before I heard my name.

"Miss Hope!" It was the little round man who worked the evening shift behind the reception desk. "I have messages for you."

I approached the desk. The receptionist took several pieces of paper from the pigeonhole marked with my room number and passed them to me. Mystified, I thanked him.

They were telephone messages, written in the varying handwriting of several receptionists. All of them said more or less the same thing: *Mr Penn wishes to speak to Miss Hope as soon as she arrives. Please could she telephone Thamesbank 067.* The messages also reported the times and dates of his calls, at least twice a day over the last three days. He had been persistent.

I went to the telephone box near the entrance to the hotel bar, shut the folding door and picked up the receiver. "Thamesbank 067," I said to the operator, and after a short silence, the phone rang in David's house. My heart raced, my hairline felt damp, the hand that was not grasping the receiver shook a little. *David, David my love, eager to see me, impatient for my return, missing me…*

"Hello?"

I was so taken aback to hear a woman's voice, I did not answer.

"Hello? Who is this, please?" she asked sharply.

"Is that … um … Mr Penn's residence?"

"It is." The sharp tone had subsided a little. "May I help you?"

I had gathered my wits. "I'd like to speak to him, please."

"Whom shall I say is calling?"

"Miss Hope."

"Very well. One moment."

I heard the click–clicking of the woman's shoes on polished floorboards, and muffled voices.

Then a man's footsteps approached. "Clara? Is that you?"

"Oh, David!"

"You got my messages, then?"

"Yes. Is something the matter? Or did you just want … I don't know, to talk to me?"

He laughed. A small, gurgling laugh like an amused child. "Of course I wanted to talk to you! My darling, I *always* want to talk to you! But yes, I suppose something *is* the matter. I'd rather tell you about it in person, though. Would you like to go out?"

"Actually, David, I'm rather tired. I've been travelling all day."

I hoped he would suggest that his driver pick me up and bring me to his house on the island, but he did not. I could hear him drawing his breath through his teeth, calculating. "Then I'll be at the hotel in … thirty minutes? Meet you in the bar."

"Who was the woman who answered the telephone?"

"My housekeeper," mumbled David, an unlit cigarette in his mouth. He took it out and removed a stray piece of tobacco from his lower lip. "Mrs Schofield. Terrible old tyrant, but she knows her job."

She had not sounded very old, but I could imagine that the woman who had spoken to me could be tyrannical. "Is it finished, then?" I asked.

He was lighting the cigarette. He looked up at me with his eyebrows raised. "What?"

"The house. Is it finished?"

"Ah! Not really," he said, and puffed thoughtfully a few times. "Mrs S. was away while the bathrooms were being done as there was no water, but she came back after Christmas to put things straight. They're starting on the kitchen tomorrow, so she'll be off again. God knows when the men will eventually quit the place. But now ..." – he gave a quick, excited smile – "let me tell you why I wished to see you the instant you arrived. I have something to ask you, and I need to be put out of my misery." He took my hand. "In the spring, when the film is finished but before I am imprisoned in the cutting room for months, I have a few days free. Would you like to come away with me? Perhaps to the seaside?" His excited look turned to an imploring one. "Please, please say yes, Clara – it would make me the happiest man alive if I could have you to myself, away from here, even for a couple of days. Will you come?"

I took his other hand and held it tight. My heart hammering, I laid my head tenderly on his chest. I did not care that we were in a public place; I did not care if the whole world knew I had found the man I loved. I was so happy I could hardly form the words. "David," I murmured, "you know I will." Raising my head, I smiled at him. "There, now. Has that put you out of your misery?"

The next morning, Aidan was in a bad mood. He argued with David, and Dennis, and even Jeanette, to whom he was usually reasonably polite. He swore under his breath during rehearsals and sometimes during our takes as well.

I was disgusted with him. I wished the filming was over, so I would never have to see him again. But I also wished the filming would *never* be over, so that I could go on seeing David every day. This conflict, and the fact that I had slept little the night before, made me grumpy too. I did not want to be under these lights, perspiring in this costume. I wanted to be in David's arms, drunk with champagne and love. By the time we had parted last night, I had made up my mind that nothing – *nothing* – would take me away from my true love. If I had to follow him from film to film across the whole world, I would. If his films were flops and he lost all his money, I would be there, ready to support him. I would bear his children and look after him in sickness and health. If necessary I would give up my life for his, like people did in stories. Our life together would *be* a story. A love story.

"Aidan, why don't you just go home?" I asked plaintively. "You're being even more impossible than usual today, and I can't stand it."

He sighed. As he exhaled, the familiar smell of whisky came to me, even though it was only eleven o'clock in the morning. "Then why don't *you* go home?" he asked illogically.

He was obviously drunk. Being drunk on the set was one of the very few reasons an actor could be released from his contract. I stepped further away from him. "You had better not let David see what condition you are in if you want to keep your job."

"I am in perfect condition," he said bitterly. "Like a well-maintained car. Or a Havana cigar." He pondered for a second. "Speaking of which, you haven't got a cigarette, have you?"

Somehow we got through that day's work. Though I was used to Aidan's behaviour by now, I suspected it was made worse by his jealousy of David. Neither David nor I could do anything to please him; he criticized my performance, David defended me, Aidan turned away in exasperation and so it went on until we were all exhausted.

I hurried to my dressing room, my nerves strung tight. "Maria, be quick," I told her breathlessly, unbuttoning my dress, my heart full of excitement at spending another evening with David. "I wish to be ready in case … anyone wants me. And I wish to get away before Mr Tobias!"

116

Half-smiling, she helped me out of my costume. She did not acknowledge my comment, though she must have been aware of the reason behind it. She might not witness much of the filming, but Aidan's dresser, Spencer, no doubt privately complained about him to her. I put on my robe and sat down at the dressing-table. "Horrid day today, Maria," I said, and reached for the cold cream.

"How much longer, Miss Hope, do you know?" she asked as she hung up my dress.

"Mr Penn says we are to finish at the end of January." I slapped cream on to my cheeks and began to smear it over my face. "If nothing goes wrong, anyway."

"Let's hope nothing goes wrong, then. I've got a job in the West End coming up."

"Oh, you're a theatre dresser too, are you?" I was interested. It had never before occurred to me that Maria, like me and the other actors, might be working for David Penn Productions only under contract and that her future was as uncertain as mine.

She nodded. Her smile had disappeared. "I prefer that work. It goes on longer than a film if the show's successful. Though it doesn't pay so well, of course."

"Of course," I agreed, though I had no idea. "Tell me, Maria…" I began, but I had no chance to finish my question, because at that moment there was a noise outside the room so loud and unexpected that we looked at each other in astonishment. I got up quickly and Maria opened the door.

The noise must have been the slamming of the heavy door that led to the area of the studios where only those with permission could go. It must have been slammed very hard indeed, because the board forbidding unauthorized personnel to enter had been loosened by the impact and was hanging by one half-hammered-in nail. While Maria and I watched, the door was opened from the other side, only about twelve inches, and slammed shut again. Very hard. The board crashed to the floor.

Suddenly anxious, I gathered my robe and went to the door. Behind it I could hear voices – masculine voices – one of them louder than the other. Then there was a thump, and a cry, then another thump. The door was opened again by an unseen hand, but before I could take a step it was slammed again with as much force as before.

Then I heard a voice. "Good God, what on earth is going on?"

Jeanette, Robert, Dennis and half a dozen other people had appeared and were standing apprehensively in the corridor. It was Jeanette who had spoken. *"That's David!"* she exclaimed, approaching the door. "Who's he talking to?"

"He's more than *talking* to someone, Jeannie," said Dennis. "You'd better stand back."

He turned the handle and leaned against the heavy door. It did not budge. "There's something blocking it," he said, his face pinched with exertion. "Come on, let's all push."

We pushed. Slowly the great door opened.

It had been blocked by a weight, a solid metal block with a recessed handle used in the studios for counter balancing the pulleys that moved overhead lights and scenery. It had been placed behind the door to stop anyone from getting in or out until the person who had put it there had finished his business.

That person, clearly, was David. On the floor lay Aidan, covering his face with his arms and swinging his legs in a vain attempt to stop the blows. Over and over again David hit and kicked him, and would have continued if Dennis and other crew members had not pulled him off.

Maria and Jeanette had their hands over their mouths. Jeanette's eyes filled with tears as Aidan rolled over, coughing and clutching his stomach. "You bloody madman!" he spluttered. "You damned near killed me! I'll sue you!"

David tried to shake off the restraining hands, and when this proved impossible he resorted, like Aidan, to verbal abuse. *"You're* the madman, you useless streak of ... uselessness!" He tried to kick Aidan in the small of the back but

119

Dennis was too quick for him and got between them. David began shouting even louder. "You've had your final warning and now I've had enough!" He lashed out again, and was again restrained. His face bright pink with frustration, he thrust his head as close to Aidan as he could get it and shouted. "You're sacked, do you hear me? You're off this film and any other film I ever make! I'll get you on a black-list! I'll sue *you*! I'll ruin you!"

Everyone started to talk at once. I stood there in my robe, with cold cream all over my face, wondering anxiously how the man I loved could be so different from last night. He looked wild, with loathing in his eyes, his clothing dishev-elled, his knuckles reddened and a bruise coming up on his temple. I did not countenance Aidan, whose punishment I was sure he had asked for. I cared for only David.

The next day David was not there. Jeanette found me alone in my dressing room at half past two in the afternoon, in full costume and make-up, waiting to start. "David telephoned," she said. "He's on his way from London and he wants to talk to us all. Could you be on the set at three o'clock, please?"

"What's going on?" I asked.

She grimaced. "He's been to see the money men."

As instructed, we gathered in the studio half an hour later. David did not sit down in the director's chair but stood, one hand in his pocket, the other holding a lit cigarette, despite the smoking ban on the set. He looked exhausted and his clothes were crumpled, as if he had not changed them from the day before. The swelling on his temple had partly closed his right eye. "Been a long night," he said, "but I've managed to get them to agree to finance the overrun made necessary by the departure of you-know-who."

There was a general murmur. "Great news, David!" called Dennis. "When's the new deadline?"

"End of February." David drew deeply on his cigarette. "Aidan's scenes are more or less complete, but we have to film long shots with a stand-in and the back of the stand-in's head to cut in with shots of people talking to him. And we'll use bits of film of Aidan's face, from try-outs and so on. It'll be tight, but we'll do it."

"Who've you got to stand in?" asked Robert. "Rudolph Valentino?"

"Gregory Wright-Hanson," said David.

A groan went round. "That *bore!*" complained Godfrey.

"He does the job," said David steadily, "unlike some

121

actors I could mention." He shot a look at me. "Clara, you'll like old Gregory."

"I hope so," I said doubtfully.

David smiled, but I could tell he was suppressing impatience. "My dear Clara, don't make yourself anxious. The film will be finished on time, and everything will be all right. Oh, and the money men have at last decided what to call the film. *Innocence*."

No one spoke.

"To reflect both the unjust beheading of Charles de Montfort and the naiveté of his lover," David added. "I think it's a pretty good title."

I did too. The thought of seeing the title on the screen, followed by *starring Clara Hope and Aidan Tobias,* thrilled me more deeply than I could admit.

"Right," said David, finishing his cigarette and stubbing it out in a coffee cup, since there were no ashtrays. "We start in half an hour. Gregory's coming tomorrow."

Gregory Wright-Hanson had been chosen for his physical resemblance, at a distance, to Aidan. But his behaviour off-screen could not have been more different. He did not forever have a cigarette in his hand, nor did he keep a bottle of whisky in his pocket. He did not amuse himself by antagonizing David. And time was not wasted while he argued or had to have his wig straightened or his nose powdered again because he had walked off the set to blow it on a borrowed handkerchief.

Furthermore, Gregory made no attempt to befriend me, advise me or take me out to dinner, but treated me with sycophantic respect. I could not even prevail upon him to call me Clara. To him I was Miss Hope, always. He repeated his lines perfectly and did everything David wanted, however many times he wanted it, without complaint. He was, as Godfrey had suggested, rather dull.

But he was pretty good at his job; once the camera started rolling, his movements were as "big" as David wanted without looking unrealistic. But he lacked something I struggled to name. Presence? Personality? Charm? Whatever it was, I missed it sorely during those final weeks. Watching the rushes at the end of each day, I noticed how much more skilful an actress I had become, so much so that having to re-do some of my scenes, and a large number of what Harry called "headshots", hardly seemed a difficult task. It was merely work. Over the last six months I had, I suppose, transformed myself from a beginner into a professional.

Aidan would be amazed. But what did it matter what Aidan thought? When the filming was over, I was going to go away with David, to Brighton for the weekend. Every time I thought about it my heart quickened and a picture leapt into my imagination. My darling David and me on our first holiday together, away from everyone, wrapped in each other's arms and enduringly in love.

The filming was completed exactly on time. On the last day of February, David threw a party at the Café Royal. Very late, as we and the few remaining couples danced to the band's final number, David held me closely and whispered into my hair.

"This time tomorrow, my darling, we shall be alone together by the sea. We had better sign the register under assumed names. How does Mr and Mrs David Williams sound? Given your lovely lilt, don't you think a Welsh name will add verisimilitude? I could always try and do a Welsh accent too, for fun."

I had not expected this. He had assured me, several times, that he was a gentleman. "Do you mean we are going to pretend to be *married*?"

"Ah." I felt his breath on my scalp as he sighed softly. "How delightfully innocent you are!"

He was right; I *was* innocent. But Florence, Mary and I knew that being married to a man involved sharing his bed and succumbing to the advances he made there. Growing up in the moral confines of Haverth, it had taken a while to dawn on me that such things also happened between people who were not married, and sometimes resulted in a girl "getting into trouble". If her baby's father did not agree to marry her, children that arrived by this means were absorbed into the girl's family. But tolerant though this might sound, shame and disapproval still attended the unmarried mother. Mam had made this very clear to me. "She's no better than she should be," she would say, shaking her head sadly when the offending female passed. "And her mother isn't much better!"

This meant, of course, that if I were to get into trouble myself, it would reflect upon Mam's upbringing of her daughter as much as on my own irresponsibility. Mindful of this, I guarded my virginity with vigilance. Eager though I was to hear about Florence's adventures with Bobby Pritchard (though where he put his hands and what she said to him was about all it amounted to) no one had ever impressed me with the desire to abandon my own principles.

But now, at least, I knew that if I were ever to permit anyone to unlock the secrets of whatever married, or unmarried, people did in their beds, that person would be David. His caresses had shown me how easy it would be to be weak, and how difficult some women found it to resist. But I knew he loved me, and we would soon be married – *really* married, not pretending, like those poor souls who conducted illicit affairs.

"But if this troubles you, then we shall not be Mr and Mrs David Williams," said David. "Why don't you be Miss Clara Williams, and I'll think of another name for myself?"

I smiled up at him. "Thank you. It is so good of you to respect my wishes."

"How could I do otherwise? Now you have made your position clear, a man would have to be an absolute cad to suggest anything else."

Eyes closed, I nestled my cheek against his chin. "We shall have a wonderful weekend," I assured him. "But morality is as important as love, you know."

These words were not my own but those of Reverend Morris, the vicar of Haverth. And he had not said them to me, but to Mary Trease's sister Megan and her husband-to-be when they had gone to receive his pre-marriage advice. Megan had told Mary, and she had reported the phrase to me. "I think the vicar's quite right, don't you, Sarah?" she'd said stoutly. "If anyone tries to get *me* into trouble, however much I love him, I'll think of the Reverend and resist!" I had agreed that I would too, and now the test had come, I had passed it. Reverend Morris, I could not help thinking, would be very satisfied indeed.

The Royal Albion Hotel was a cream-painted building among other cream-painted buildings on Brighton sea-front, not far from the oriental-looking structure known as the Royal Pavilion. It too was cream-coloured. And that March day, a stiff wind moved the clouds around in a cream-coloured sky above a grey sea. There were no leaves on the trees, and the people who passed had their overcoat collars turned up and their hats pulled low.

"It's not much like Aberystwyth," I observed as the taxi drew up.

David laughed. "Why on earth should it be?"

Aberystwyth was the only seaside resort I had ever visited. Aberaeron, our nearest town, was by the sea, but it was just for fishing. No one would ever want to stay there for a holiday. "Mm." I was uncertain. "It looks almost like London, with all these big buildings but with the sea along one side. And it's all whitey-cream, like … I don't know, a wedding cake?"

He looked at me quizzically. "You do say the most extraordinary things sometimes, Miss Williams." He gave some coins to the taxi driver. "Keep the change," he told him, and the man touched his cap and drove away. "Brighton's a large town, certainly," continued David, "and, of course, it has a reputation for certain things."

"What things?"

The doorman signalled to a porter, who picked up our bags. As we followed him between the columns each side of the hotel entrance, David took my arm. "Racketeering," he whispered. "It's known to be full of criminals, so look out for dubious types."

"Not in a hotel like this, surely?" I asked, dismayed.

"Hah!" His eyes glittered, but he did not seem very amused. "Well, even in a hotel like this, or perhaps *especially* in a hotel like this, the clerk will know that for every 'married' couple that register, another dozen will not be married at all."

"How shocking!"

"That's the other thing Brighton's famous for, you see. You'll remember to sign your new name, won't you?"

While David was busy at the reception desk, I looked round the foyer, impressed by its elegant furnishings. Though slightly old-fashioned, even to my uncritical eye, the Edwardian splendour of the hotel's interior added to my excitement. I felt thrilled at the thought of being in a town well-known for adulterous liaisons between people rich enough to afford the Royal Albion. Mam and Da and Frank and Florence and Mary were at home, celebrating St David's Day with daffodil buttonholes and *bara brith*, just like they had done every year for their whole lives. Even if they wondered what I was doing, I was confident they would never guess that I was in an opulent hotel, about to sign my name for discretion's sake, as Clara Williams!

It struck me that Clara Williams was my newest name out of three. On Monday I would go back to being Clara Hope. Would I ever go back to being Sarah Freebody? I smiled furtively, dipping my chin into my fox fur. Sometime in the future David and I would stand before Reverend Morris in the village church and swear to love and honour one another for ever. And I would have yet another new name.

I hovered over the register. After a moment's hesitation, under David's signature, which read *D. Mitchell-Drew*, I signed *C. H. Williams*, with a little flourish at the end like a pig's tail.

"Rooms 255 and 256, sir," said the clerk, handing the bell boy the key. "Would you like to order dinner or breakfast, or morning newspapers, or an alarm call?"

I hoped David would order all these things, except the alarm call. I was about to speak, but he brushed the man's words aside. "No, nothing. Come along, Clara."

We followed the bell boy into the lift and up to the second floor. After a few steps along a carpeted corridor, he opened the door of room 255 and stood back. I entered a pretty, but not particularly luxurious, room. There was no balcony, though the tall window did look out over the sea.

"You take this room, my dear," said David. He asked for my bag to be brought in and for his own to be put in room 256. While I waited for him to tip and dismiss the bell boy, I went to the window and parted the lace curtains.

Across the street from the hotel the Grand Pier jutted into the sea. Ice-cream men and ticket sellers stood at its entrance, but business was very slack. It was too cold for trippers.

And the pier, I noted, was painted cream.

"This place should be called *Cream*ton, not *Bright*on," I said to David, letting the curtain go. "Though I suppose when the sun shines on all this cream paint, it *does* look quite *bright*."

Suddenly he was very close behind me. I could feel the warmth of his body. "Have you finished talking drivel, dearest?" he asked playfully. "Because if so, I have other employment for you."

I turned, and put my hand on his chest. His shirt felt damp. I wondered why he was so hot when the room was cool enough for me to be comfortable wearing my fox fur. He tried to kiss me, but I pulled away. "David, are you all right? You seem so hot – perhaps you have a fever. Oh, I hope you're not going to be ill!"

"Of course I'm not going to be ill. I do feel warm, though." He smiled his most sensual smile. "I must be fired with passion, my darling."

"Then you may kiss me when I have cleaned myself up a little." The train journey had made me feel grubby, though I had bathed that morning. "Where's the bathroom?"

He released me, looked round the room and opened a door in the corner. It led to a narrow bathroom, old-fashioned like the rest of the hotel but containing the essential fittings. Opposite the door was another door, bearing a brass number, 256. "Oh!" I exclaimed in surprise. "The bathroom is between our two rooms!"

David was feeling in his pocket for his cigarettes. "Clever, isn't it? That's why I booked them. Better than tiptoeing down the corridor to the bathroom in the middle of the night." He paused to light up. "The sooner European hotels start putting a private bathroom in every room, like they do in America, the better."

I could not imagine a hotel with as many bathrooms as bedrooms. It seemed impossibly extravagant. "I don't think that will ever happen," I told him doubtfully. "But yes, it is nice to have a bathroom just for us."

He exhaled smoke. "I'm going across to my room now. You're right, we could both do with a wash and brush-up. Get changed too, and we'll go out and find some dinner. Knock when you're finished, will you?"

He kissed me swiftly on the cheek, unlocked the door that led to his room, gave me a mock-salute with the hand that held the cigarette, and disappeared. I put my case on the bed and undid the catches. On the top, wrapped in tissue paper, lay a new silver-beaded gown. I took it out and held it against me, humming happily. Mr Mitchell-Drew and his companion, Miss Clara Williams, were going to be the smartest couple in Brighton tonight; David had said so when he had presented me with the dress on the last day of filming, describing it as an "end-of-picture gift". David never seemed able to admit that he bought me beautiful things merely because he wished to.

I laid the dress on the bed and used the bathroom, then I knocked on David's door. "All yours!" I called.

There was no answer for a few seconds, then I heard a muffled sound, which I took to be his acknowledgement of the empty bathroom. I went back into my room and closed the bathroom door, unbuttoning my blouse, my mind busy, wondering which shoes out of the two pairs I had brought I should put on for dinner. Would we be dancing? Should I wear the more comfortable pair?

I took off my blouse and skirt, and pulled up my petticoat to take off my stockings. But as I took hold of the fastenings on my suspender-belt, there was a sudden noise, and a flash. And there, in that ordinary room in an old-fashioned hotel in a place that should have been called Creamton, my world ended.

The flash dazzled me. Gasping, I put my hand up to shield my eyes. A man had flung open the door from the bathroom: a man in a dark overcoat and trilby hat, with a camera round his neck and a flash bulb in his hand. I drew breath to scream, but someone came up behind me and put their arm round my throat. A strong, masculine arm. I was dragged backwards towards the bed, pushed down and held there. Astoundingly, the man pinning my shoulders to the pillows was David.

"What are you *doing*?" I demanded, half-blinded by the curtain of hair that had fallen over my face during our struggle. "Call the manager! This man is a criminal! Call the police!"

The man had a straggly moustache and looked unwashed. I was sure we had fallen victim to one of the "dubious types" David had warned me about, an obvious blackmailer. But David didn't seem to care. He kicked my suitcase and the silver dress to the floor, his face grim, perspiration gleaming on his forehead. "Shut up!" he hissed.

"He's not a criminal, you little idiot!"

"But—"

I was silenced by his hand over my mouth. It was then I realized that he did not have his shirt on. His braces hung loose, and the top button of his trousers was undone. Real fear gripped me; my body seemed cold and unaccountably heavy. Again I tried to scream but produced only a sort of whimper. "If you make a sound," David told me, "I'll turn you out into the street, half naked or not."

He took his hand away from my mouth but grasped my face between both his hands and pressed his lips to mine. I heard the *click-squawk* of the camera, and there was a flash. "Got that one, sir," said the man.

Strain as I might, I could not move. David's superior weight and strength held me where I was. He pulled down the straps of my petticoat. Another *click-squawk*, another flash. He grabbed me by the elbows and thrust my arms around his waist. Before I could retrieve them, there was another *click*, another *squawk*, another flash. I tried to sit up; again and again David pushed me down.

"Got enough, I think, sir," said the man, lowering the flash bulb.

"Good," said David. "Now get those developed straight away. I'll be in touch."

The man disappeared into the corridor, shutting the door softly behind him. David swung his legs off the bed

135

and began to button his trousers. "God, I need a drink."

I had been too shocked to cry, but now the tears came. "David, will you *please* tell me what's going on?"

He looked down on me, his face dark with some elemental force I could not recognize. Even his rage when he had attacked Aidan had not shown itself like this; this was a mask of triumph and loathing, like a man would turn on his defeated opponent after a bloody battle.

"Get up and get dressed," he commanded. "I don't care where you go, just get out."

"David, I beg you, tell me … what have I done? Have I displeased you?" A sob came into my throat and almost choked me, but I blurted the question I had to ask. "Don't you love me any more?"

These words only increased his fury. "Shut up, you stupid little fool!" he commanded. Then he seemed to soften a little and between heavy breaths said, "Go away and read your contract. If you try to breach it I will sue you."

I was still sobbing. "But I don't understand," I protested weakly. "David, please tell me—"

"For Christ's sake! Do you think I've taken all this trouble for my own amusement?"

"I do not know what to think." My brain felt useless, stunned.

"Well, I haven't." David's voice was shot through with misery. "I've done it to get rid of that bloody woman."

The memory of Marjorie Cunningham's cap of golden hair flashed through my head. I gasped for breath. "What woman? Do you mean Mar—"

He ignored me. "Of course, the court case will provide free publicity for the picture too, and keep those damned sharks off my back."

"What court case?" I was wailing now. "David, please…"

"The *divorce* case, you fool!"

I gasped, silenced by bewilderment. I had never felt my ignorance so keenly. Whose divorce case did he mean?

"Don't sit there gaping like a fish," said David. "Here." His jacket lay on a chair. He searched the pockets, his fingers trembling so much that his wallet got stuck as he tried to pull it out, and in his irritation he tore the pocket flap. He tossed a five pound note onto the bed beside me. "Now, get out of my sight, and don't come near me again until your contract says you have to."

Even now, it is painful to write about the events of that evening. My heart, still full of the torment David Penn inflicted upon it, will not settle. The words live on the page, pulling me back down into that darkness, as unwelcome memories always do. I wish, despite all that has happened since, that I had never agreed to go to Brighton with him. I wish I had been more suspicious of his too-ready acceptance of my insistence upon separate rooms.

I had been more innocent even than he knew. I had believed, with a naiveté beyond comprehension, that a man would take a woman away for the weekend and be content to meet her each morning in the dining room for breakfast and say good night outside her bedroom door. It still makes me blush to imagine what the hotel clerk must have thought when we registered as an unmarried couple and took separate rooms, albeit with a shared bathroom in between. That we were cousins? Or perhaps colleagues on official business? Or that Miss Williams must be an imbecile? David had called me a "little idiot", and he was right.

I sat on the bed for a long time, my tears drying on my cheeks. I wiped my eyes and looked at my fingertips; they were smeared with mascara. My actress's eyes must be a sorry sight. But I could not bear to get up and inspect them in the mirror. I did not want to look at myself. I felt too numb to do anything.

I still did not truly understand why David had done what he had done, but it was clear that I was now mixed up in the sort of affair that was discussed in Haverth only in whispers and never in mixed company or in front of children. There would be two versions of what had occurred in this room tonight – David's and mine – and no one would believe my version. It would be the word of a ... what did people call it? ... a *floozy*, against that of a rich, respected film director. A floozy was an ignorant girl who went with men in order to get nice things – oh God, the bracelet! The dress! The dinners at the Ritz and the Café Royal! And in many people's minds, as Florence had reminded me, an actress was little better than a prostitute.

I went on sitting there, my dismay increasing. How I wished I had taken more notice of my contract! By agreeing to its terms, whatever they were, I had taken a step into the hidden undertow of a world neither I nor my family understood. But there was no retreating now. I could not face my parents and Frank, and especially Mary and Florence. I could never go back to Haverth and be Sarah Freebody again. And how could I face Jeanette and Maria and Dennis, and all the other film people who knew David and whom I had trusted as I had trusted him? I could not go back to the Thamesbank Hotel and be Clara Hope either.

So where *could* I go?

My wristwatch said seven minutes to eight. Wherever I decided to go, I had to set off soon or it would be too late to get a train. My head heavy with crying and confusion, I hauled myself to my feet. Slowly, without looking at my half-dressed state in any of the mirrors in the room, I took a clean blouse and a pair of stockings from my case and put them on.

Once I was wearing my skirt and jacket again, I took up my hairbrush and sat down at the dressing-table. In my reflection I looked bony and black-eyed, like a small animal chased to the point of exhaustion, waiting for the hounds to gather for the kill. I began to brush my hair, moulding the waves round my fingers, musing on the fact that I was not a beautiful actress at all. I was the unfortunate victim – quite possibly deservedly so – of a confidence trick, and I certainly looked the part. Dejected, years older than my age, wondering if I could ever again believe what anyone said.

I took off the make-up round my eyes and did not renew it. But I decided to put on lipstick, as my lost alter ego, Sarah Freebody, had always done. Suddenly, I wondered what had happened to that stick of lipstick from the chemists in Aberaeron, the first and only one Sarah had ever bought. Was it still in my make-up bag? I had an overwhelming desire to find it.

The bag, a quilted satin one I had bought in Selfridges the same day as my fur, lay in a corner of my case. I rifled it desperately, hoping for a sight of that familiar brass tube. It was not there. I tipped the contents of the bag out onto the dressing table. Compacts, bottles, boxes and jars clattered on its glass surface. My old lipstick wasn't there, but my eye caught a crumpled piece of paper with something written on it. Puzzled, I picked it up. *23, Raleigh Court, Bayswater, London W2.*

I read it twice, and realization dawned. This scrap of paper had been in my make-up bag since that day when I lay in my dressing room, suffering from my first hangover. Without doubt, the address belonged to the person who had written it: my erstwhile leading man, Aidan Tobias.

I stared at the cigarette paper. It was such a small thing, so thin it was almost transparent, and the ink Aidan had written the words in was smudged and discoloured from its long sojourn among my cosmetics. But it was a miracle that it was there at all. Why had I not thrown it away as soon as Aidan had left the room that day? Contemptuous of him as I was, what had made me keep the paper? And what had he said as he had written on it? I closed my eyes and searched my memory. He had wanted me to take care. "Do not disregard yourself," he had said, with a sadness I had not understood.

I opened my eyes. Aidan had said something else that day. He had told me not to disregard "some people" who cared about me, which I had assumed meant himself. Knowing he was jealous of my affair with David, I had dismissed his words. But now I remembered them clearly. "They will be there if you ever need their help."

Aidan was the very last person on earth I wanted to see. Normally I would have run as far away as possible from his voice saying, "I told you so". But things were not normal. With one stroke my journey away from Sarah Freebody towards a wise and sophisticated Clara Hope, capable of enchanting both David Penn and the cinema audience, had been derailed. I could not go in either direction, but I could not stay where I was either. However wary events had made me, I would have to take Aidan at his word. At least for now.

I put the paper in my jacket pocket, crammed my hat on my head, touched my lips with lipstick, packed my case, picked it up along with my handbag and fur, put the key on the bedside table and left the room. I did all this as quickly as I could in order to stop myself thinking. I had to get out of the Royal Albion, and, for good or for ill, Aidan had offered me an escape route.

In the corridor, I pushed the door to the stairwell and listened. The only sounds came from the dining room, where dinner was in full swing. I felt I would rather die than pass by the reception desk, with the clerks smirking and whispering. As quietly as I could, struggling a little with my case, I went down the stairs. At ground level there was a door bearing a notice saying *Fire exit only. Please keep locked.* My heart sank, but when I tried it I found it had the kind of lock you could open from the inside, but not the outside, without a key. Limp with relief, I twisted the latch, slipped through the door, pulled it behind me and stepped into the darkness.

Victoria Station was as busy as usual. By the time the Brighton train arrived there the clock on the station forecourt said twenty to eleven. The ticket collector asked me if he should summon a porter, but I refused, embarrassingly aware that the five pounds David had given me might be the last money I acquired for a long time. So I carried my own case to the taxi rank.

The night was cold, with that smoky edge London air always seems to have. Crowds of men and women, bundled in fur collars and gloves, their breath misting, flowed in and out of the station entrance. Ahead of me in the taxi queue, a couple no older than myself stood close to each other, her arm through his, their faces pink with expectation. Where were they going? Where had they come from? Why were they so happy? I tried not to look at them. The sight of all these people doing whatever they were doing on a normal Saturday night, laughing and talking and being with each other, deepened my already bitterly low mood. I dug my feet into the pavement and my hands into my sleeves and wished to die.

"Where to, miss?"

The young couple had gone off in their taxi, and the next one had drawn up. "Oh ... Raleigh Court, Bayswater, please. Number 23."

The driver hopped out, put my bag in the luggage compartment and hopped back in again, whistling. I thought how uncomplicated being a taxi driver must be, and for a moment I actually envied him. But when the cab swung into the traffic, my envy disappeared. I realized I had never been in a London taxi alone at night before. David had always been there to chain my attention, so I had never been aware of the swarm of motor cars and horse-drawn vehicles, bicycles, motor bicycles, double-decker omnibuses and hackney cabs swirling along the streets. It all looked so higgledy-piggledy, and there were so many lights and conflicting noises, I wondered how the driver could work out what to do and where to go without injuring himself or me. Rounding Hyde Park Corner, I was thrown sideways even though I was holding tightly to the strap above the taxi door.

I am alone, I said to myself. *I am grown up. For the first time in my life there is no one to do anything for me; there is only me.*

As the taxi slowed down, the driver looked from side to side of a narrow street, searching for number 23. I began to panic slightly. Supposing Aidan was away, or not in, or refused to answer the door?

I leaned forward and spoke to the driver. "Excuse me … could you please wait? The person I am visiting may not be there."

"Very good, miss."

In order to deposit my case at Aidan's door, the driver had to come into the light that shone above it, and I saw for the first time that he was young. I started to envy him again. Much later tonight he would count his takings and go home to his mother or his wife. Tomorrow he would go out, perhaps to a football match. And tomorrow night, if anyone cared to look, they would find him as usual outside Victoria Station, ready for drunks, complainers, arguers… How lucky he was in his ordinariness! As I thanked him I noticed he was quite good-looking. I wondered bleakly if he would ever appear on a newsreel and be "spotted" for the films.

When I rang the doorbell, footsteps sounded inside the building. The taxi driver tipped his cap. "That'll be one-and-ninepence, miss."

I gave him two shillings. "Keep the change," I told him, as I had heard David do. He touched his cap again before he returned to the waiting cab. And at the same moment the door of number 23 opened.

"Good grief!" Aidan stood there with one hand on the door latch and the other in his pocket, his eyebrows in his hair. *"Clara?"*

"Good evening, Aidan. May I come in?"

In the train I had rehearsed the speech I would make to him. But now it sounded prim and spinsterish, as if I were an aunt addressing him in an I'm-determined-to-educate-you tone.

He gave one of his exaggerated stage bows. "By all means, madam." He caught sight of my suitcase. "And you've come to stay! How positively *de-licious!*"

The spinster aunt vanished. "Shut up, Aidan, and help me with this, will you? I've had a long day and I'm exhausted."

Grinning, he picked up the case. "Well, at the risk of offending madam, I must say you look it." With his other hand, he pulled me into a small vestibule, from which rose a flight of polished wooden stairs. "This way."

I went up first. As the front door crashed closed behind me, something like the fear I had felt in the hotel room overwhelmed me. We were only halfway up, but my legs failed. I stopped and turned helplessly to Aidan, whose bemused expression immediately changed. "Clara, whatever

147

has happened? You look ..." – his eyes roamed my face – "has someone hurt you?"

He was a blur. I do not know if it was tears or faintness that dissolved my image of him, but I could no longer support myself. I had escaped from the hotel, found Brighton Station, caught the right train, taken a taxi and arrived at 23 Raleigh Court, fired by determination not to allow David's betrayal to defeat me and by my habit of imagining I was someone else, in this case a taxi driver. But now that I had caught hold of a lifebelt – Aidan was at least familiar, and he was *here* – I suddenly found myself nearer than ever to drowning.

Aidan caught me around my shoulders and lowered me to a stair, where he sat beside me while I wept. The weeping became howling, and still he sat there calmly, comforting me with soft murmurs as one would a child, tolerating my shoulder-shaking sobs and dripping nose. When the flood lessened, he took a clean handkerchief from his pocket and wiped my face while I hiccupped and sniffed. "Oh, dear ..." I blurted apologetically, "what must I look like?"

"You look like a girl who's been badly hurt by some heartless bounder," he said. "And I'm pretty damned sure I know who. Now come in and make yourself comfortable."

He helped me to my feet and up the rest of the stairs. From the doorway of the main room I could see that the flat was the home of a man who cared little for wealth but a great deal for comfort and beauty. There were no thick carpets or silk-upholstered chairs; rather, the comfort of a soft sofa and the beauty of book-lined walls. I had never seen such a room. Since I had left Haverth, I had lived in hotels. I had only seen decoration designed to impress rich people who had the same sort of furnishings at home. But Aidan's sitting-room, simply furnished and softly lit, had no pretensions to impress anyone.

The floor was polished wood, over which had been laid a rug. Not the Persian kind with intricate patterns I had seen in so many hotels, but a plain rug, the colour of grass. In fact, the exact colour of the hills around Haverth in the first days of spring. At the windows, which were the old-fashioned sash kind, were cotton curtains, unswagged, untrimmed, unfringed, and the colour of the sky on the hottest summer day. Apart from the sofa, there were cushions on the floor and a wicker chair. The only wall not covered with bookcases was crowded with pictures: photographs of Aidan and other people, sketches, postcards, greeting cards, some framed, some not, some not even mounted but stuck to the corners of others with drawing pins. I gazed and gazed.

My legs were trembling. I was glad Aidan was still holding on to my arm. "Is this really where you live?" I asked.

"What an odd question!" He gave me a puzzled, but amused, look. "Do you think I merely *pretend* to live at 23 Raleigh Court, when my true home is far away in … I don't know, Ruritania, perhaps?"

He was right. It was a foolish question. But I was foolish enough to be taken aback at the sight of a modest, pleasant room after months of lying in starched sheets gazing up at ornate ceilings. "I'm sorry," I said, hoping he could hear that I was sincere. "It's just very different from everywhere else I've been since … well, since I left home."

I could not go on. My throat contracted, and I bowed my head, unwilling to allow Aidan to witness yet more tears. I swallowed repeatedly, trying to compose myself.

Aidan had the decency not to look at me. He settled me in the corner of the small sofa, bustling a little, asking if I were warm enough and could he get me some tea or something to eat?

"Please don't take any trouble." My voice was a whisper. "I am quite all right."

"I've got some soup I can heat up," he said, halfway to the door that led to the rest of the flat. "And I'll do some bread and butter, shall I? And tea. I could do with a cup myself."

He brought me a bowl of soup and put a plate of bread and butter and my teacup beside it on a low table, then sat in the wicker chair, balancing his own teacup on his knee, and regarded me carefully. "Now, are you going to tell me what's brought you to my door?" After a pause, he added, "My *real* door, that is, not the one in Ruritania?"

I did not smile. "Thank you very much for this." I took a mouthful of bread and butter. "I had no supper." I took another mouthful. "What brought me to your door, as you say, was the piece of paper you wrote your address on, ages ago. It was in my make-up bag, all screwed up and dirty. But I could still read it." I took a spoonful of the soup. It was too hot but unexpectedly delicious. "This is very good."

"It's only some vegetables and a bit of stock."

I looked at him sharply, wondering if it was another joke. I had never heard of a bachelor, or indeed any man, making soup. He looked back at me with an expression of innocence. "Do you think I can afford a cook? I can make eggs and bacon, too. And lamb chops. I assume my cooking skill is the sole reason you turned up here, since I am accustomed to being roundly despised by Miss Clara Hope."

I stirred the soup and blew on it, giving myself a little

time, collecting the courage I needed to admit the truth. "I came here because I have nowhere else to go," I told him. "Perhaps you remember that you once offered me help if I ever needed it? Well, I do."

For the first time since my arrival, I looked at him, properly. His hair had been recently washed but not oiled, and stuck up in tufts at the back, as if he had been resting it on a cushion. It was now almost midnight, so he might have been in his bedroom when I rang the doorbell, though he was dressed in old trousers and a shirt without its collar on. On the front of his pullover I detected a cigarette burn, possibly two, and a smear of something like gravy. His face looked just as it always did – self-aware, mocking, alert, smooth. The injuries David had inflicted upon it had healed. I had never noticed before how slim his shoulders and chest were. Or had he got thinner since I had last seen him?

"So what has David done?" he asked.

"I don't *know*," I confessed. "I don't understand. All I know is that he has broken my heart."

He sighed softly. "Oh, Clara. You're a nice, loving girl with no experience. A blank canvas for David Penn to put whatever he likes on."

I could not dispute this. "He said I'm an idiot."

Aidan made a sound like *Grrrumph!* and said, "Only an idiot would consider you an idiot, Clara."

"So *David's* the idiot, then?" I took another spoonful of soup. "Aidan, please let's be serious. I am more of an idiot than you suppose. You see, when David asked me to go away with him to Brighton for the weekend, I didn't realize he meant I was supposed to, you know …" – I could feel myself blushing helplessly – "share his bed."

"Ah," said Aidan with resignation. To my relief, he did not try to make a joke.

"And he'd booked two rooms, because I'd insisted. But there was a bathroom between them, with a door from each room." I paused. "I suppose it was easy for someone to hide in there."

He frowned. "Someone was hiding in the bathroom?"

"I know it sounds like something from a penny dreadful," I said, still red-faced, "but there was a man in there, and when I was changing he suddenly came into my bedroom, and he had a camera and he was taking pictures of me without some of my clothes on."

The room was utterly silent. By this hour the residents of

153

Bayswater had retired. The window must have been open; a breeze twitched the blue curtains. Aidan whistled softly. "Christ, Clara."

"And do you know what happened next? David came in through the bathroom too, and he wasn't wearing his shirt, and he pushed me onto the bed, and..." Unable to go on, I put down my spoon. I got up and looked at the bookshelves through watery eyes, trying not to sniff, hoping Aidan would have the grace to let me gather myself.

But he finished the story for me. "And the man took photographs of you both, on the bed, and David made it look as if you were lovers." He was on his feet at the gas fire, lighting a spill, fumbling for his cigarettes. "Didn't he?"

My embarrassment silenced me.

"Clara..." He pondered for a few moments while he lit the cigarette. Then he said in a quiet voice, "You might not understand why David did this, but I think I do. Do you remember what he said to you, if anything? Did he threaten you, for instance?"

"Not threaten, exactly. But he mentioned a woman, and a divorce. And he told me to read my contract and not come near him until it says I have to."

Aidan looked at me with a sort of half-nervous delicacy. "Ah. Well, it seems to me that the photographs were taken to be used in evidence in a ... um, a divorce case, as you say."

As he said this, suspicion fell on me, and crushed me. "Aidan, whose divorce are we talking about?"

His face was troubled. He took a quick puff on his cigarette, then another one. "Look," he began, "I am sorry to bring you this news, but as I think you've guessed, the divorce in question can only be that of … David himself."

I stared at him. "So … just to be clear … you're telling me that David is *married*?" Anger and embarrassment heated my cheeks and made my heart thud. "Why on earth did no one think to tell *me*?"

Aidan looked profoundly unhappy. "Clara, I swear I did not know, and I'm sure no one else did either. But secret marriage or not, it sounds like he is desperate to get out of it and has involved you in a set-up."

"What do you mean, a set-up?" My anger was subsiding, but my embarrassment had increased.

"Well, you see," continued Aidan, "if a man and his wife wish to divorce, there must be *grounds* – cruelty, abandonment, and so on. The easiest one to get away with is adultery, but there has to be proof that one of the parties has committed it. Private detectives in places like Brighton do thriving business 'catching people at it'. Sometimes it's real – the wife hires the detective to follow the husband and photograph him with his lover. But usually it's agreed between the wife and the husband that he will lure an unsuspecting woman into bed with him, or even hire a prostitute, so that his real mistress's name can be kept out of it."

My heart was still beating very fast. *Thud, thud, thud.* "So …" I ventured in a small voice, "are you telling me that David not only has a wife, he has a mistress as well?"

"Oh, Clara!" This was uttered as a sigh. "There is more between David and Marjorie than the Atlantic Ocean, you know. They are lovers, and have been for years."

Thud, thud, thud. Aidan's tone was not patronizing, but full of sympathy. He took a resigned breath, and went on. "David has done this so that *your* name, rather than Marjorie's, will be mentioned in court. You see, a correspondent has to be cited for the grounds of adultery to be proven, and the divorce to be granted. And the photographs do prove that you were there, in a hotel room with David, don't they?" He considered a moment. "Indeed, the only grain of truth in this whole sorry tale is that *you agreed to go away with him for the weekend.* And how fortunate for him that you did! The little scene he was planning could not be set in motion without its leading lady, could it?"

Thud, thud, thud. I pressed my fingers to my forehead, as

if I could erase my discomfiture by force. No wonder David had been so anxious to secure my agreement! Leaving messages for me at the hotel, rushing to meet me there as soon as I telephoned. And I had thought it was because he was besotted with me! I tried to breathe steadily, but it was no use. I took a few quick steps about the room, my shoes clicking on the polished floor.

"Aidan, for pity's sake, why did you not tell me the truth about Marjorie when I asked? Of course it would have been heartbreaking, but since my heart is broken anyway, what does that matter? I would not have gone to Brighton, and everything would be all right!"

I thought he would apologize, but all he said was, "For heaven's sake, sit down. You're making this look like one of David's ghastly theatrical scenes; 'pace about agitatedly, move stage left, say your line, move stage right, adjust the curtains to show nervousness, move stage left, sit down again…'"

"Stop it! Will you just *stop* it!" I cried, as theatrically as any director might wish. "This may be a big joke to you, but to me it's the…" I floundered for words. "It's the end of everything. It's the end of *love*." My voice faltered. My chin dropped onto my chest. "I was sure David loved me, as I loved him. I know he has wronged me, but I cannot forget what happened between us and how he made me feel." I raised my head and looked at him steadily. "Aidan, haven't you ever been in love?"

He did not answer. He smoked to the end of his cigarette, stubbed it out and lit another, his face so consumed with concentration I wondered if he had forgotten I was there. I sat down on the edge of the sofa, like someone expecting bad news. Finally, Aidan turned to me. His eyes contained a thoughtful expression; I could not guess what he saw in mine.

"Yes, I have been in love," he said. "I too have discovered that even if the object of one's passion does not return it, the passion remains unaffected. And even if they misbehave, it is not automatically extinguished. Love is not subject to the usual rules of engagement. It is not organized, like war between nations, or a game of cricket. It is the stirring of deep emotions and includes the pain of having them stirred."

My heartbeat had slowed during his silence, but now it gathered pace again. I had never heard such words from him before. The grip in which he usually held his feelings had loosened: now, perhaps, whatever lay in his heart was on the edge of release.

"Of course," he went on, "I understand that an attachment such as you felt for David cannot vanish upon the instant of betrayal. And I am contrite at my flippancy. It is a habit of mine to joke in order to avoid admitting some things are serious. I should curb it, I think." Unexpectedly, he took my hand. His touch was familiar from the many times we had been in a "clinch" on the film set. I was comforted by it. "I must impress upon you how deeply I regret keeping the truth from you," he continued. "But I had no idea of the depth of your feelings for David, or that things had gone so far with him. I imagined, along with everyone else at Shepperton, that it was a flirtation." He was smiling one of his humourless smiles. "Actually, I did broach the subject with Robert once, but he said, 'My dear boy, if the director's having a bit of fun with the leading lady, that's hardly news, is it?' And he was right, after a fashion. It was not my place to preach to you, so I said nothing."

I was too crushed to speak. Aidan took a long drag on his cigarette and thought for a moment, then he added, "If we had known he was married, you may be assured we would have warned you." He gave me a rueful look. "They may be louche, or degenerate in their habits, or vain, and they are definitely tiresome, but film people are generally more moral than they would have you believe. And I did, if you remember, ask you to be careful of yourself."

"But I did not understand what you meant!" I protested. "I assumed you were jealous!"

"So you thought I had designs on you myself?" He blinked rapidly while he breathed smoke. Crestfallen, he let go of my hand. "You must have a very low opinion of me."

I did not know what to say. My opinion of Aidan had been revised so many times in the last hour, I no longer knew what it was. "I just wish you'd *told* me," I said softly.

"So do I, Clara," he said with feeling. "God knows, so do I."

Aidan insisted I sleep in the only bedroom, while he settled down on the little sofa – uncomfortably, I was sure. I slept as if I had been beaten over the head and left for dead. Aidan did not wake me. When I eventually appeared in the sitting-room at half past twelve the next day, bathed, and dressed in my only remaining clean blouse, he handed me a buff envelope and said, "Have a look at that while I make some breakfast. Then get your hat and we'll go out, shall we?"

I went to the window and looked at the street, which daylight had revealed to be a mews behind large houses, narrow and cobbled, with a gutter down the middle. The envelope, which was unsealed, contained a collection of folded papers. The stiff cream paper reminded me of the correspondence I'd received from David Penn Productions, and when I held the title page to the light I realized why. In my hands was Aidan's contract.

"Why have you given me this?" I asked when he came in with a tray of tea and toast.

"Because I'm assuming you haven't got yours about your person." He put down the tray and straightened up. "You didn't drink the tea I made for you last night, you know. Don't you like my tea?"

"Oh … last night!" I shrugged helplessly. "I was beside myself. I did not know what I was doing. The tea was probably as delicious as the soup, but I forgot all about it. Sorry."

Aidan smiled, and nodded towards the contract in my hand. "I reckon your contract is much the same as mine, though you probably get paid more than I do. You said last night that David told you to read your contract, so maybe if we read mine, we can work out what he meant."

This was obviously a good idea. "Thank you, Aidan," I said, hoping he would believe I was sincere. "You've helped me more than you needed to, you know."

He put his hands in his pockets and raised his thin shoulders in his nervous way. "I believe our American friends would say 'Aw, shucks, ma'am' in this situation. So put it on the table and let's look at it."

161

He poured the tea and we began to read through the contract, sipping solemnly, nibbling bits of toast. I could not understand any more of it than my own. "It's all in legal language," I said. "You'll have to tell me what it means."

"I'm not sure I know," mused Aidan, scanning the pages. "But the bit I'm looking for … ah, this might be it." He put down his cup and used a corner of his slice of toast to point to a section at the bottom of one of the pages. "Here. I bet you've got the same clause in yours. I am under contract to 'make such public appearances as deemed necessary by the producers for advertising purposes'," he read. "And in fact, Clara, since I signed this, I've had to sign another agreement to the same effect or risk being sued. I was only sacked from the filming, not the subsequent appearances for advertising purposes."

I looked at him, stricken. "Public appearances! What does that mean?"

"Well…" He finished his toast and began to collect the pages. "Attending the premiere, for a start."

"But I have no intention of attending the premiere! I never want to see David again. And how can I face anyone else who worked on the picture? Jeanette, and Robert, and … oh God, *Simona*! I wish the whole film could be destroyed and thrown in the rubbish bin!"

Aidan's face looked thin and hungry, and his eyes narrowed. "You cannot mean that. And anyway, you have no choice. If David's wife cites you as the object of his 'adultery', it will be all over the newspapers. The story has everything they adore: money, sex, beautiful people and just the right touch of sleaziness to titillate the masses. It will be the biggest scandal of the year. The public will flock to see *Innocence* so they can nudge each other when you appear on screen and feel superior to this woman of no morals who will sleep with someone else's husband. You will be mobbed at the premiere. And your future career as an actress will be assured."

I was horrified. David knew the scandal would help publicize the film. His betrayal had wounded me deeply, but this was worse. He was prepared to sacrifice an ignorant girl at the altar of greed so that he and his money men would be welcome in America. Unlike me, he could leave behind everything he no longer wished to be associated with: Clara Hope, the divorce, the scandal … and his wife.

His wife. Who was she? How long had they been married? Why did they wish to divorce? Did she know about me? Had I actually seen, or even meet her, among those bejewelled butterflies who fluttered around David with their flat chests and flat hair and kohl-rimmed eyes?

"Oh, Aidan." I folded my arms on the table and put my head on them. "I wish I were dead!"

"No, you don't." He hauled me to my feet. "Come on, a breath of fresh air will do you good."

An insistent March wind blew as we crossed Bayswater Road and entered Hyde Park. We walked necessarily briskly, I with my gloved hands tucked into my coat sleeves, Aidan with his hands in his pockets, both of us with hats pulled down over our foreheads.

The trees along the edge of the park were bare. The sky was white, brightening occasionally, but holding the threat of rain. It reflected my gloomy mood. We walked in silence for a long time, my mind busy. My usual strategy of pretending to be someone else failed me; I thought only of my folly and its consequences. Aidan had been kind, but I could not expect further help from him. And whatever happened,

I would have to leave 23 Raleigh Court as soon as possible. Unmarried women did not stay with unmarried men, even under ordinary circumstances. With the threat of public scandal hanging over me, it would be another piece of dirt the press could dig up on me. And, unforgivably, on Aidan.

Horrified by this thought, I must have gasped, because Aidan slowed his pace. "Am I going too fast? Sorry."

We had come to a bench, so we sat down. I put my chin into the collar of my coat so that he wouldn't see my agitation. "Aidan," I began, "I have decided what to do."

"Hah! Doesn't involve murder, does it?"

"No, it involves some sensible behaviour, for a change."

Grimacing, he took out his cigarettes. "Good God, sensible behaviour? How tedious!" He tapped a cigarette on the packet, but didn't light it. "So what is it?"

"I can't stay at Raleigh Court any longer. You can't know how grateful I am to you for putting me up, but tomorrow I'll be on my way."

He frowned, the unlit cigarette still between his fingers. "May I ask where you intend to go?"

"Well, David gave me five pounds, and I've got money in the bank and in a trust my father opened for me, so I'll look for a room to rent. David Penn Productions are still paying me, so I'll be all right."

"I see. And what will you do?"

"What I should have done in the first place. Go to the police."

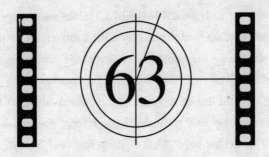

He lit the cigarette and smoked absently, his eyes on the faraway trees. I waited for a few moments, but he did not speak. Feeling uncomfortable, I busied myself adjusting the angle of my hat.

"Clara, listen to me," he said at last. "I insist that you and I rub along at Raleigh Court for as long as necessary. This is not your Welsh valley, this is Bayswater." He considered. "Well, the edge of Maida Vale actually, so that's even better. No one gives a damn who an actor has in his flat."

"But when this … this story gets into the newspapers," I protested, "imagine what they'll write about us!"

Aidan looked amused. " 'Leading Man and Leading Lady in Love Nest!' It even alliterates!"

"Please, I'm serious."

"I know you are, but so am I." He had stopped smiling and his eyes had got narrow and flinty. "The story, as you call it, may never even get into the newspapers."

"Exactly!" I was relieved that he had understood. "That's why I'm going to the police! I know they won't believe my

166

word against David's, but at least I'll have done the right thing, won't I?"

"Whether they believe you or not, there is no point whatsoever in going to the police," he said, not condescendingly but merely as a matter of fact. "Their job is to solve crime, and I'm sorry to have to tell you that in this instance no crime has been committed."

I was nonplussed. "But the man was hiding in the bathroom!"

"Had he broken into the bathroom through the window?"

"No, of course not. David had let him in."

"And did David attack you, or threaten you with a weapon?"

"No, but he—"

"Pushed you down on the bed, pinned your arms behind you and kissed you passionately?"

"No! Well, that may be what it looked like, but..." Dismay swept over me. "Oh."

Aidan spoke gently. "The private detective who took the photographs, and who, incidentally, is without doubt well known to the Brighton police, was simply doing his job. David paid him, quite legitimately, to provide evidence in a divorce case. What is *really* between the two people in the photographs is of no interest to the detective, the police, the lawyers, the judge or anyone else. Evidence is the only thing that counts in law."

"But … even if the photographs enable David to get his divorce, surely they will ruin *his* reputation too? He is in them, after all, half naked on a bed with a girl!"

Aidan moved a little nearer to me. "Clara, this is how it works. In cases such as these, the girl is condemned as a scarlet woman, but for the man, especially a man like David, the whole thing merely adds to his glamour. It's a phenomenon of civilized life that you may have heard of. It's known as the double standard."

I looked dejectedly at the muddy lawn that spread before us. It reminded me of the fallow fields around Haverth. But thinking of Haverth hurt my heart. "So there is nothing I can do. David will get away with it, and I will be ruined."

"Not necessarily." Aidan dropped his cigarette stub and ground it out with his toe. "When I said the divorce case might never come to court, it was because we might be able to stop it. Don't laugh, but I think I've got an idea."

Aidan's shoulders looked high and tense. His fingers drummed the bench between us. He was looking at me with his actor's face – eyes alight, forehead a little puckered, mouth slightly open, as if he were about to kiss the heroine. "You see, the photographs will be sent to David's wife, who will give them to her lawyer. After that it'll be months before the case comes up. We've got time to do something."

I was dubious. "Aidan…"

"Don't worry, I'm not going to get your hopes up, then disappoint you. By the way, did I tell you I've got a part in a new picture?"

"No, you didn't. And what about your idea?"

"I'm telling you about it. When I've finished this picture, I thinking I might jack acting in and do something else."

I was surprised. "But you're really good!" I said truthfully.

"Well, thank you for that." He smiled one of his I'm-not-really-smiling smiles. "I had no idea you even noticed my acting."

He was right; I had considered him a nuisance and treated him with impatience. I had taken my cue from David, whose contempt for Aidan was obvious from the first day. Aidan's behaviour, on and off the set, had automatically irritated me because it irritated David. I had fed my own vanity by assuming Aidan was jealous of David, without bothering to wonder if there might be some other reason for the friction between the two men.

I was embarrassed. Aidan was still the man I knew, with his actorish gestures and affected phrases, who smoked and drank too much, but since I had descended upon his flat he had conducted himself impeccably. "Um … I notice lots of things," I said weakly.

He put his hands in his pockets and looked at me sheepishly. "You see, I'd rather be a photographer. That's what I'm really interested in. I like to think I'm pretty good at it." He smiled thinly. "And David isn't the only person in the world who can set up photographs that are not quite what they seem."

I felt suddenly anxious. "What do you mean? No, I know what you mean. You are going to get photographs of David in a compromising situation with a young girl, aren't you? But how will that be of any use? What about the double standard?"

"You are quite right. But the photographs I am going to get will not involve David and a girl. They will show him with something else entirely."

I did not feel any less anxious. "This isn't going to involve anything fishy, is it?"

"Fishy?" His voice was low, but I heard the anticipation, and, strangely enough, a note of compassion in it. "Clara, listen. Have you ever heard of something called cocaine?"

My voice came out very small. "No, I don't think so."

"Thought not." Aidan stood up suddenly and pulled down the brim of his hat. "Look, can we walk a bit? I'm getting cold."

We set off in the direction of Park Lane. "Don't alarm yourself," he said, "but cocaine is a drug made from the coca tree, found in South America. It's not used for medicinal purposes, though. People – rich people, as it's very expensive – use it to make themselves feel good."

I was not alarmed, but interested. "Like wine and cigarettes?"

"Exactly, except that alcoholic drink and tobacco are legal, and cocaine is illegal. You can be arrested and imprisoned for possession of it, and if you are caught importing or selling it you're in very deep trouble indeed."

My interest increased. "Are you telling me that David uses this thing? Cocaine?"

"Yep," he nodded, "along with the rest of his set."

"What do they do with it? Drink it? Smoke it?"

"No, it is taken through the nose. They sniff it."

"And they risk getting caught just to feel good?"

"It's fashionable." He gave a small shrug. "It's what the people David wishes to impress do. And like cigarettes, the more you have the more you want." He looked at me squarely. "Believe me, Clara, I'd never touch cocaine myself. I much prefer the old cigs, and whisky, of course. But people like Marjorie Cunningham are so dependent on cocaine to keep themselves happy, they cling to David because he knows where to get the stuff."

A memory rose up, and I gasped. "Oh!" I stopped so suddenly that a man in a top hat bumped into us. He apologized, raised his topper and went on his way while I stared at Aidan, stricken. "That's why you thought it was funny that I should imagine Marjorie had come to David for a job. She had come to him for cocaine, hadn't she?"

He let his expression be his answer. I went on standing there, my brain busy. "So you are hoping to photograph David sniffing this stuff?" It was like a script from a film. Trying to control my voice, trying to be as nonchalant as Aidan, I pressed on. "And … you will tell David that you'll give the photographs to the police unless he destroys the photographs taken in the hotel?"

"Exactly." Aidan's eyes had begun to glow a little. He began to walk on. "We'll catch him unawares. You'll set up the photograph, and I'll take it. All you need to do is what you've been doing for the last six months. Act."

I had been cold, but now I was hot. I dragged my fur from around my neck, my face suddenly burning. My legs felt weak, and I sat down where I was, on the steps of a drinking-fountain. Aidan sat down one step lower, so our faces were on the same level. "I can't do that!" I hissed.

"Why not?" His face had its hungry look. "You're the obvious person to do it."

I drew the fox's body backwards and forwards between my hands, feeling its softness, wishing as ever that I was someone else. That nanny in her olive-green uniform, hand-in-hand with a toddler. The man running to and fro on the grass with a kite string in his hand, watching the kite dance in the sky with more interest than his small son. Any of the stone figures that adorned Marble Arch. "Aidan, you know very well why not. Acting with a script and a director is one thing, but this is real life. It's *deceiving*, which isn't the same thing at all."

"But David deceived *you*!"

"Exactly!" I said irrationally. "And if I go anywhere near him, he'll treat me just like he did in that hotel." My voice began to waver a little. "I can't go through a scene like that again. I don't know David. I don't know *you*. I'll never be able to decide whether anything is fact, ever." Inexplicably cold again, though the sun was strengthening, I put my fur back on. "Don't you understand? I'm *scared*."

"Clara, if you would just try and understand…"

"I *do* understand!" Tears smarted behind my eyes. The events of the last twenty-four hours had left me as battered as if it had been me that David had kicked to the ground, not Aidan. "Look, Aidan, I am not a …" – I struggled for the word I wanted – "a puppet, or a doll or something, with no feelings. I can't turn on David and give him a dose of his own medicine, as if he meant nothing to me. He *does* mean something to me, as I thought we established last night."

"Please hear me out, Clara, I beg you…"

I stood up. Park Lane swam before me. I blinked and it recovered its clarity. "No, I won't. I don't want to hear any more about this. Thank you for everything, but I am going back to the flat now to pack my case."

"Don't be ridiculous." Aidan got to his feet. "You don't know the way back, and anyway you haven't got a door key." He took my arm, and as he did so, the first drops of rain began to fall.

When we got back to the flat, the sitting-room was almost dark. Aidan lit the gas lamps on the wall and blew out the match, his eyes on my face. I bustled about, unbuttoning my gloves and unclipping the fox's tail from its mouth, taking off my hat and patting my hair. "My feet are freezing. Might I have a bath before I go?"

He went on looking at me, the spent match still in his hand. "Clara, you're not going anywhere. Please, stop this silliness and listen to me, will you?"

"Silliness!" I was incensed. "Why am I being silly because I have refused to be party to pointless revenge? Why can you not admit defeat?"

He patted his pockets for cigarettes, retrieved a crumpled pack and searched it.

My patience broke. "And why must you *smoke* all the time?"

He found a cigarette and lit it, his eyes still on me. The smoke made a blue stalk in the air. "We all have our vices," he said steadily. "And in answer to your other question, I cannot admit defeat because what I am proposing is not 'pointless revenge'. It is an opportunity to do something that should have been done – *I* should have done – a long time ago." He took a shaky breath, and his face took on a stubborn, determined look. "Clara, I must tell you that you are not the first to suffer at David Penn's hands. But if you help me now, hopefully you will be the last."

Illuminated from behind, Aidan's features were almost invisible. And it seemed to me in that moment that everything else about him was invisible too. Who was this man? In the months we had worked together on the film, through all the scenes we had rehearsed and filmed, our physical proximity, our shared exhaustion, he had cultivated an air of cynicism, even arrogance, as if everyone else was a child and he an adult. He had behaved as if treating it all as a joke was the only way he could survive. Perhaps it was. His offer of future help, which I had not even understood at the time, remained the only chink in the door he kept so tightly closed.

As I stood there in my stockinged feet, coat and fur over my arm, my anger subsided. "Why do you care so much?" I asked softly. "If I end up being cited in a divorce case and am branded a … what did you call it? … a scarlet woman, then that does not affect you at all. If I do not agree with what you propose, what does that matter to you?"

He went to the window. The curtains were not yet drawn. He looked down to the street, but it was clear that he was not seeing it. After three or four puffs, he began to speak in a sort of distracted murmur, as if he were talking to himself.

"If I tell you what I know about David, you will understand. Did you know his real name is David Penhaligon?"

I thought of Mr Reynolds, my old schoolmaster, instructing us in English about the British Empire, and my da at home, using his mixture of Welsh and English to tell me about the British government's attitude to Wales, the Welsh and our ancient language. Cornwall had an ancient language too, and "pen" meant "head" in both of them. I wondered, randomly, if David knew that.

"No, I didn't."

"They are a family of criminals," said Aidan. "His father's been in prison for years, and his mother went off with someone else. He started in films as a runner, a messenger boy, and because he's good-looking he got taken up by a rich woman and taught manners. She gave him money to start his company. But then of course he dropped her as soon as he began to be successful."

I tried to digest what he was saying. "But how do you know all this?"

"Because…" He sat down on the sofa and reached for the ashtray. "She was my mother."

I was so surprised I could not move. I remained glued to the middle of the green rug, feeling its pile through the soles of my stockings, thinking uncontrollable thoughts about people's mothers, and my own mother, and betrayal, and the fight between David and Aidan, and the sorrow and shame of ruined reputations. I tried to say something sympathetic, or at least not too crass, but I had no breath to speak.

"I was employed on the first film David was the AD on, about five years ago," continued Aidan. "He latched on to me, I suppose, because I was better educated and better connected than he was, and he hoped to raise himself up by clinging to my coat-tails. He met my mother because she used to like to come and watch me on set sometimes in those days. He fawned over her, and she was so lonely – my father had died two years before. She was flattered and was forever telling me how kind and wonderful he was. But I never trusted him and he knew it, though he maintained a polite façade. He couldn't stand the fact that I saw through him. I knew he was an opportunist and a liar, persuading my dear Ma into giving him money while carrying on with God knows how many other women, sniffing cocaine and keeping every champagne producer in France in business."

My surprise had been replaced by a nervous, unsettled feeling. Robert Palliser had suggested I invite my own family to tour the studios. If I had, who could say what influence David might have exerted? The thought of my impressionable brother falling under his spell terrified me. "So…" I began slowly, considering each word, "your revenge would not be pointless. But it would still be revenge."

He sighed, and passed his hand over his forehead. "Yes, I suppose so." Agitated, he was smoking fast.

I watched him in silence while his cigarette rapidly diminished. "May I ask … what happened to your mother?"

"Oh, she drowned." He said this matter-of-factly. But the gaslight revealed that every tendon in his neck, in its stiff collar and tie, was tight, and perspiration filmed his upper lip. "Apparently, she fell off a ship. But whatever they say, Clara, I am convinced that in actual fact, she jumped."

My hand went to my mouth, and I let out an involuntary whimper.

"You see, after David left her," he went on, "she was never the same. Someone suggested she go on a cruise. For a relaxing holiday, I suppose. I waved goodbye to her at Tilbury, and the next time I saw her was in the mortuary."

My body felt as if it had been winded by a severe blow. But my limbs had recovered their ability to move, so I sat down beside him, and with the small amount of breath I could muster, I asked, "But how can you bear to be anywhere near David, after what happened?"

"Well, of course I swore I would never work with David Penn again, but financially, needs must. I hadn't worked for months and months, and when the job on *Innocence* came up, my agent urged me to take it. He doesn't know about David. I wavered, then when I heard that a new young actress was going to play the lead I decided to do it." He took a few pensive puffs. "I thought I would be able to manage for the sake of a starring role, but I couldn't. You saw what it's like between David and me. And when he started getting his claws into *you*, imagine how I felt."

He stubbed out his cigarette and lit another. I had never seen him chain smoke like this, though the reason for his excessive drinking and smoking was becoming much clearer. "Clara, I know all this is in the past," he said decisively. "I know that preserving your honour will not restore my mother's and will not bring her back to me. Above all, I do not wish you to think you have gone from being deceived by one man to being forced into something against your will by another. But David Penn has not reformed. If we do not do something now he will go on considering himself above the law, just like his father did before he discovered he wasn't and ended up in jail." His voice softened a little, but his expression remained unyielding. "Do you not see? By helping me do this, you will make David think twice before he tries to ruin someone else."

Now I knew the reason behind his warning that day in the dressing room. *Be careful of yourself*, he had said. His mother had not, perhaps, been careful enough of herself. "Oh, Aidan…" My feelings had rolled themselves up into such a tight ball that my stomach ached. Instinct made me lean against him, my head in the hollow under his chin. "I understand. This is vital, isn't it?"

Like a string unravelling, the tension left his body. I could feel the drumming of his heart. He put his arm around me and squeezed my shoulder. Emotions and memories crowded within me: Da, my dear silly old Da, had always squeezed me like that when I did something he approved of, like coming first in a spelling test at school. Frank, who rarely touched me, had put his arm around me as we stood together at Grandma Freebody's funeral last year. I had been sobbing; he was prevented from doing so by the necessity of appearing manly. But his emotion flowed down his arm; I felt it, just as I felt Aidan's emotion now.

"It's the most important thing I've ever done," he said.

My decision seemed to make itself. "Then tell me what you want me to do, and I'll do it."

FINAL REEL

ACTION

I had nothing to wear. I had packed for two nights in Brighton: two clean blouses, a spare slip, a nightdress, two sets of underwear and the beaded evening dress. The silver evening shoes and bag I had brought to go with it were hardly suitable for going about London in the daytime, so I had no change of shoes. I had no cardigan or sweater to put over my silk blouses, only my tweed jacket and skirt, and a raincoat. And I had run out of stockings, though a pair I'd rinsed out in Aidan's bathroom were drying on the curtain rail in the bedroom.

"Aidan," I said sheepishly the next morning, "I need some clothes."

He gave an exaggerated moan and clapped his hand to his forehead. "Of course you do!" He began to gather his wallet, cigarettes and outdoor clothes in a businesslike way. "Look, we've got to go to Somerset House this morning anyway, so let's go via Oxford Street and buy you some new things. And we need to go to the post office in Trafalgar Square when we've finished all that, so I'll set up

185

a poste restante address and we can get your possessions sent from the Thamesbank."

I had so many questions. I did not know which to ask first, so I said nothing.

"Come on, get your hat," said Aidan, already halfway out the door. "We'll have some breakfast on the way. Do you like muffins?"

I followed him down the stairs, struggling into my coat. "But I haven't got all that much—"

"Don't worry, I can write a cheque." He stopped, one hand on the door and the other held up, palm out. "And don't say, 'Oh, Aidan, you mustn't!' I know you don't want to be beholden to me, and you're not. You can pay me back when you are able. Now, come under my umbrella. It's raining stair-rods out there."

The Aidan of last night, who had so openly laid bare the painful events of his past, was gone and the playful façade had returned. His feelings were back in the place he normally kept them: locked deep inside his heart. I felt privileged to be one of the very few who had glimpsed something more profound. "Thank you," I said. "Thank you for everything."

He took a large black umbrella from the stand, opened the door, crammed his hat on his head and regarded the weather with a grimace. "And thank *you*."

He took my arm and we hurried out of Raleigh Court and into Bayswater Road, huddled under the umbrella.

"What are you thanking me for?" I asked. "I haven't done anything."

"Of course you have!"

"What?"

"Well, Miss Clara Hope…" He paused while we crossed a busy road, dodging puddles and horse dung. When we got to the other side he pulled me so close I could feel his breath on my face. "The clue is in your name. You've given me hope, Clara. Hope that there may be an end to the guilt David Penn's conduct has inflicted on me. Or at least" – he pushed the door of a café advertising freshly baked muffins – "a lessening of it, which is probably the best I can get."

I looked out of the cab window at Oxford Street; it was not very crowded on this Monday morning. The shop windows spilled light onto the wet pavement. Selfridges, where I had purchased the fur and several evening dresses, seemed to stand in blank-faced admonishment of my folly. I turned to Aidan. "Let's go down to Marshall & Snelgrove, shall we? They have nice dresses and things, not too expensive." I regretted this as soon as I had said it. "Not that I mean, you know…"

"It's all right." He patted my hand. "I'm not completely broke, actually. And anyway, I've got this new job."

"Oh, yes!" I had forgotten that Aidan had a part in a new film. "You must tell me all about that!"

"I will, but let's get you kitted out first."

He bought me two medium-weight wool dresses, some underwear and stockings and an adorable vertically striped cardigan with a deep V-neck. It was pricey; I tried not to show Aidan how much I liked it, but he saw through me immediately and insisted on buying it. Once we had added a nightdress and a pair of soft leather pumps, the amount rung up by the assistant was alarming. Aidan paid without comment, and it was not until we were back out in the street that either of us spoke. We began at the same time, then stopped, then both tried again. Aidan laughed. "You first."

"I was only going to say thank you, again, and promise you again that I will pay you back."

"And I was going to say that you will need some more clothes soon. Summer ones."

"But my summer things will be sent from the Thamesbank, won't they?"

"Yes, they will." It had stopped raining. He used the furled umbrella to hail another cab. "But they might be

188

too warm for where you're going."

I did not understand. "I'm not going anywhere."

"Yes you are."

The cab stopped. "Somerset House," said Aidan to the driver. Then, to me, "That's where they store the records of births, marriages and deaths."

"I know that. So where am I going that will need cool clothes?"

"Italy."

"Italy?"

He helped me and my packages into the back seat and squeezed into the small remaining space. "It's a place in Europe. It looks like a boot."

"Aidan, do not tease me, just tell me what you mean!"

He sat back with satisfaction and took out his cigarettes. "My new film is being made on location, which means the outdoor scenes will be filmed in a real place, out of doors. And that place is … Italy."

I was so surprised that if I had not been wedged into the corner of the taxi, I might have fallen on the floor. "So do you mean we could have gone to Paris and filmed our outdoor scenes?" I gasped. "Instead of pretending, with those stupid painted walls?"

"No, no!" Aidan shook his head. "David Penn Productions has not the funds for location filming; it costs an absolute fortune. But the director who's making this picture, Giovanni Bassini, is very keen on filming outdoors, and his backers seem to have tons of money."

I had begun to recover my composure. "So it's like when the newsreel people came to Haverth, is it?" I ventured. "They brought their cameras, and lights and cables, and goodness knows what."

"Yes, but this is on a much larger scale. The film company won't cart all the stuff over to Italy, they'll hire an Italian company's equipment."

I stared at the back of the cab driver's head without seeing it. My mind was crowded with so many thoughts and questions, it was hard to find a sensible way through them. "So where exactly are we going?" I asked eventually.

"To Castiglioncello, on the north west coast of Italy. Giovanni, who is a *very* good friend of David Penn, has a villa there. If there's one thing David likes to do when he's finished a picture, it's to be entertained at Giovanni's villa. I would stake my life on his turning up there before long."

"And where do I come in?"

"You will be introduced as my Welsh cousin, who has come to Italy to learn Italian." He gave me a shy look. "I'm afraid, Clara, you will actually have to do so, for verisimilitude. And no one in Castiglioncello, except David, of course, will know who you really are."

"*D*avid Maurice Penhaligon, bachelor, to Catherine Ann Melrose, spinster, in the parish of St Pancras, fifteenth of June, 1915*," read Aidan. "His age is given as twenty-four and hers as eighteen." He turned to me. "Good grief, Clara, *eighteen*!"

This fact had hit me so hard, it was colouring my face. I said nothing.

"That was eleven years ago," observed Aidan thoughtfully. "So she's twenty-nine now, and he's thirty-five."

Thirty-five. Almost twice my age. To cover my confusion, I bent over the entry in the register more closely. And something caught my eye. "Look at this, Aidan. It says that David was born in London, but Catherine Melrose was born in New York, and her address at the time of her marriage was in West 86th Street. She's American."

We looked at each other, and I saw realization in Aidan's eyes. "So he married an American citizen and scuttled off to the USA, did he?" He gave a soft, humourless laugh. "Well, in 1915 that was an excellent way to avoid being conscripted into the forces! And I thought he'd just bribed someone!"

My discomfort had increased. "Aidan," I confessed, "I am so very ashamed of myself."

He hurried to comfort me. "Nonsense! David is the one who should be ashamed of himself! And he does look younger than his years. I would have put him at no more than thirty-one or -two, and I've known him much longer than you have." He heaved the enormous book closed. "Anyway, it's hardly your fault that he likes girls who are much younger than him. Lots of men do," he said seriously. "I mean, I'm forty-two, and here I am in Somerset House with an eighteen-year-old girl."

I smiled weakly. "How old are you, really?"

"Twenty-five on my birth certificate, twenty-three to the public. I split the difference and consider myself twenty-four."

"Oh!"

We had begun to make our way to the exit. I followed Aidan between shelves and desks, tiptoeing on the polished floor. The Public Records Office wasn't a library, but it looked and felt like one.

"You sound surprised," he said. "Did you think I was older, or younger?"

"No, it's just…" What was it? Aidan sometimes seemed much more than twenty-five, and sometimes much less. He had his drawn, serious face and intense looks, but when he was charming people and making them smile, he seemed no older than me. "I just never really considered it, that's all," I ended lamely.

A current of cold air came in as Aidan pushed the heavy door open. "Hold on to your hat," he said, turning up his collar. "Raining again. Do you think you can walk? It's not far. Or shall we get another cab?"

It wasn't raining much, though it was windy. "Let's walk," I said. "But where are we going?"

"The post office in Trafalgar Square. If you're going to come to Italy, you'll need a passport."

I had never known anyone who had a passport. There was not much call for such things in Haverth. The wind was blowing my fur against my cheek and disarraying my hair. "Aidan, slow down, I'm getting out of breath. Do you mean you get a passport from the post office?"

"No, you get a form and fill it in," he explained, shortening his strides. "Then some other people need to write things on it and sign it, and then it's sent to the Passport Office. Since you're under twenty-one, one of those people will be your father."

"My father! But how can we explain to him why I'm going to Italy?"

"Don't worry," he said airily. "It's perfectly natural that you might have to go abroad to film some scenes. You haven't told your parents it's all finished, have you?"

"I don't think so. I can't remember."

"Well, no matter. If you have, we can always say 'something came up', which is what people always say when they don't wish to explain."

I considered this. "But that would be lying, Aidan. To my family."

"Oh, not really. A bit of constructive vagueness can be useful sometimes."

It did not take long to get a passport-application form and establish a poste restante address.

"Miss Clara Hope, Post Office Box 3353, Trafalgar Square, London WC2," I read from the paper the assistant gave me. "Sounds very grand."

"It isn't," said Aidan, ushering me towards a table. "People have been using poste restante addresses at hotels and post offices all over the world for centuries, to hide their whereabouts, or their identities, or their infidelities, or their criminal activities…"

"Romantic, then," I suggested.

"Quite."

We sat down and I began to fill in the form. *"Sarah Harriet Freebody,"* Aidan read over my shoulder. "Your real name is much nicer than mine. Who would wish to be called Allan Turbin? I used to be nicknamed 'Dick' at school, as it's so like Turpin."

"I hate Harriet," I told him. "It's my granny's name on my mother's side. She's always called Hetty, which isn't quite so bad."

"And Sarah?"

"Mam's name." I concentrated on writing, trying not to think about Mam. "I much prefer Clara."

"So do I," he said, with enthusiasm. "Though I'll have to get used to calling you Cousin Sarah when we're in Italy, won't I?"

I smiled. "So shall I call you Cousin Allan, then?'"

"You'd better not!"

When I had completed as much of the form as I could, Aidan bought a sheet of writing paper and an envelope, wrote a letter to my father asking him to ensure the rest of the form was completed as soon as possible, put everything in the envelope and sealed it. "I'll send this registered post," he assured me, "so if it gets lost we'll know. And if it doesn't get lost, you'll soon be the owner of a little navy blue booklet with a number stamped on it and the Royal Coat of Arms. A British passport opens doors across the globe, you know."

I did not need to open doors across the globe; all I needed to do was travel to Italy under my real name. "How long will it take?" I asked. "To get the passport?"

"A couple of weeks. And you need photographs too." He scrutinized me sideways. "If I were you I wouldn't wear all that slap. And put up your hair. The less like Clara Hope you look, the better."

When we got back to the flat I spread my purchases out on the bed. Although they were lovely, especially the striped cardigan, it gave me an uneasy feeling to see them lying there, waiting to be worn and admired. David had bought me things, spending money for no other reason than to woo me and use me for his own ends. I wondered if I would ever wear the beaded dress or the bracelet again. I was so glad he had not bought me my beloved fox fur! But the clothes spread before me now, which Aidan had paid for without demur, served to point up the difference between the two men. Aidan seemed to care nothing for the trappings of the film business, which were so important to David. Aidan lived modestly, employing no housekeeper, possessing no motor car. His clothes were good but few, and some of them were so old they made him look quite poverty stricken. He smoked and drank, that was true, but not cigars and champagne. He didn't go to nightclubs or casinos and had seemed uncomfortable that night at the club, and not just because Simona had been flirting with him. It was as if he wished to distance himself from the unabashed acquisition, and display, of wealth.

And yet he must come from a wealthy family. I pondered over this. David had ruined Aidan's mother in more ways than one; he had taken her reputation and her fortune. I thought about the cruise she had been on when she died. "Someone suggested" she take it, Aidan had said. Had the "someone" also paid for it? What had she felt like, boarding the ship at Tilbury, embracing her son, then watching him go back down the gangplank and join the crowd on the dock to wave goodbye?

What had been in Aidan's mind, and in his heart? Did his disgust with David extend to disgust with the entire business of acting and making films to the extent that he was considering giving up altogether?

There was a knock on the door and I heard Aidan's voice. "Are you changing, or can I come in?"

"Oh, I'll come out!" I began to fold the new clothes back into their tissue paper. If he saw them arrayed like this, he might think I was as obsessed by clothes as the people he despised. "Just a minute!"

When I opened the door I noticed he'd gone into the kitchen, where he stood with a bottle of wine in one hand and a glass in the other. "I would have brought this to you in your boudoir, madam, you know," he said with the sort of arch look beloved of stage actors. "Madam likes red, does she not?"

"Yes, please."

I perched on the kitchen stool, hugging my knees. I had to make myself as small as possible because the kitchen was not designed to contain more than one person at a time. Aidan poured us each a glass of wine and held his up. "Chin chin." We clinked glasses. "To Italy."

We drank. The wine was strong, but delicious. I took two more sips. "Right," said Aidan. "I'm Sergeant-Major Tobias, and you're Private Hope. Here's the drill."

"Drill! You're too young to have been in the war."

"I spent the war in a boarding school, for heaven's sake. Do you think we didn't have drill?"

I tried to imagine what Aidan had been like as a schoolboy. I would have been a very little girl. "So while I was learning my letters and knitting socks for Our Boys in France," I said, "you were practising to *be* one of Our Boys."

"But luckily the war ended before I had to go, thank God."

I thought of the memorial in Haverth that bore the names of sixteen young men from the parish who had given their lives in France. One of them was Mary Trease's half-brother. When the telegram had come, the loss ceased to be personal to the Treases and became that of the whole village. Robert Trease had been killed early in the war; as more and more families were bereaved, and fiancées robbed of their marriages, all we prayed for was the end.

"Ready?" said Aidan. "I'm Signor Lingo, the proprietor of the language school. I speak English, of course, but only just." He cleared his throat and took on his character. "So, Miss Freebody, you wish to have Italian class? I am so very honoured! But please, you tell me why you come to Castiglioncello?"

"Um… My cousin, Mr Tobias, is acting in a film being made near here. We have taken an apartment in the town, and I shall be keeping house for him. As we are to be here for some time, I wish to learn to converse with Italian people."

"Very good," said Aidan. He poured some more wine into his glass and held out the bottle, but I shook my head.

"And, Miss Freebody," he went on, still as Signor Lingo, "may I ask what you do when you are not learning of the Italian here with us? You have free time? You like to come out with me to swimming, perhaps?"

I was frowning at him, my glass halfway to my mouth. "What?"

"I'm trying to be authentic," he said. He put down his wine glass and shrugged, spreading his hands. "We poor men, we see bee-oo-ti-ful lady like you and we cannot help ourselves. You come to beach with me?"

I took a sip. "You're serious, aren't you?"

"Just warning you. Italians are well-known for being Casanovas, as I'm sure you know. They'll try it on with you, Clara, every single one you meet, so I hope you're ready."

"Well…" I was not sure what to say. "I'll have to be, I suppose."

He had taken up his glass again and was looking into it, swirling the wine around moodily. "You see, what I'm really trying to say, in my clumsy way, is that I don't think you realize how very, very *attractive* you are. To men, I mean." His cheeks suddenly flushed. I was intrigued; I had never seen his composure disintegrate so suddenly.

"Obviously, David's eye was caught by your astonishing beauty on that newsreel, and, to give him his due, he also recognized talent in you. But every man on that film set would have courted you if he could. Well, except Dennis, but that's another story. The only reason they kept their

hands off you is that David already had his hands *on* you."
He had recovered enough to look at me with glowing eyes.
"Believe me, Clara, beauty is a gorgeous thing, but it can
be a weapon, too. And in the end, when you've fought off
God knows how many Italians, you're going to have to use
that weapon against David."

The kitchen was silent. I sat there on the stool, and Aidan
leaned against the stove. We regarded each other warily. I
had begun to understand what he was saying to me but was
not sure I wanted to. "You mean, I must use the fact that he
finds me so attractive to…"

"To weaken him," supplied Aidan. "And when he is
weak, we will be strong."

My knowledge of Italy came from a school atlas. The
capital city was Rome, and I could envisage roughly
where Venice was. But the north-west coast was uncharted
territory to me. Aidan mentioned a place called Livorno –
Leghorn in English – and told me that Pisa, with its famous

leaning tower, was not far from where we were going. In fact, we would be changing trains at Pisa station. But I was unable to imagine it until he retrieved a large book from the bottom shelf of the bookcase and flipped through it until he found the page he wanted.

"There," he said, placing the open book on my lap. "This picture is of Lerici, the place where the poet Shelley lived a hundred years ago."

The book was called *In the Footsteps of Poets and Artists: A Traveller's Guide to the Mediterranean*. I stared at the picture he had pointed out. It showed a painting depicting a scene in a village. There were small houses and a dried mud track scored by carriage wheels. People went about their business: a woman with an armful of washing, a man with a fishing net. It looked to be a port about the size of Aberaeron, but any similarity between the two places ended there. The sky was painted in Della Robbia blue – the colour of the virgin's robe – a blue so intense it was almost purple. The light seemed to come from a brighter heaven than the one above us here in England, turning the buildings and their shadows to chessboard blocks of white and black. In the corner there was a glimpse of a sparkling sea decorated with small fishing boats.

I looked up. "But this is only a painting," I said doubtfully. "It can't possibly be like this in reality."

"I assure you it is! Why else would poets and writers and artists adore it so? Italy, the French Riviera, Greece,

202

Spain ... the light of the Med is quite different from our northern light. It warms not only the skin, but the soul, I can tell you."

"No wonder David likes going there."

"Quite. And not only David. Places like Italy and Greece are good for making films, for the very same reason: the sunlight. There was a community of artists fifty years ago in Castiglioncello, but now it's more a community of film-makers. They've all got their villas there, not just Giovanni. It's rather a fashionable place, full of Americans. Hence the language school."

I read the caption beneath the picture. "Ler-iss-ee, on the Lig-oo-rian coast, by Sir Henry Fox, R. A., 1911."

"Not bad." Aidan twisted his neck to look at the picture too. "It's Ler-ee-chee, but you did well with 'Ligurian coast'. Liguria is the part of Italy where Castiglioncello is situated. South of Lerici, but still on the coast, in a little bay."

I imitated his pronunciation. "Casti-yon-chello?"

"Bravo! Someone told me once that Welsh and Italian have a historical affinity. Or was it Spanish? At any rate, you'll be speaking Italian like a native before you know it."

"With the help of Signor Lingo, of course."

We smiled at each other. Aidan's hair fell over his fore-head. He was relaxed and seemed as happy as I was to be sharing a drink in his kitchen. Perhaps it was the sight of the emptying bottle that prompted me to ask a question I had been contemplating. "Speaking of David…"

"Which we weren't, were we?" He gave me an indulgent look, as if I were a child in need of gentle correction. "And if we were, let's not, shall we? It's such a tiresome subject."

"But I have something I must ask you." I had begun to know Aidan well enough to understand that his flippancy almost always hid true concern and that he would listen to me if I persevered. "Tell me, did you ever go to David's house on the island?"

His mouth tightened so slightly that it was almost imper-ceptible. He pushed back his hair thoughtfully. "Are you quite sure you wish to know?"

This disconcerted me. "Why should I not?" Then I thought of something. "If you mean he takes cocaine there, that doesn't matter. You told me you never touch it, and I believe you. But I would love to know what the house is like. He couldn't take me there because the whole time we were working on the film the house was being remodelled. He'd recently bought it, he said. Sometimes he stayed there, but other times he stayed at his club."

He looked at me, lips slightly parted, his wine glass forgotten between his fingers. "So that's what he told you, is it?" The space between us in the small room was only the length of his arm. Still watching me, he reached out and placed his palm on my cheek. His voice was low. "Clara, the whole time we were working on that film, David, Marjorie and that whole ghastly set were hopping in and out of each other's beds in that house. It's called 'Le Grenier' or some damned silly French name. And he's had it for ages. I've only been there once, years ago, before David and I became enemies. It's nothing special, just a sort of bungalow. And it certainly hasn't been renovated in the last fifty years."

I looked down at the book on my lap. "So Mrs Schofield doesn't exist, then?"

"Who?"

We caught the train to Dover, where we boarded what seemed to me an enormous ship, as impressive as an ocean liner, though Aidan said it was only a cross-channel ferry. But I was fascinated and awed by the *Maid of Kent*. It was too windy and wet to stay outside on deck, so Aidan led me down some steep steps to the first class lounge. It resembled a hotel foyer, carpeted and surrounded by large windows. Nestled in a chair as close to one of these windows as possible, I pressed my nose to the glass, eager to take in everything that passed.

Not much did. The windy weather whipped the waves into spray, riming the windows with salt. I saw some brave people battling to walk the deck but did not envy them. "Probably sick," said Aidan when I pointed them out. "Fresh air apparently helps the old *mal de mer*. Do you feel all right?"

"Perfectly, thank you."

"Then you won't mind if I smoke?"

It was unusual for him to ask. "Not at all."

When he was settled with his cigarette, I picked up the copy of the *Tatler* magazine that had been left on the table for the occupants of the first class lounge and began to flick through the pages. It was a magazine for rich people, full of photographs of society women in ball gowns. I liked to look at the fashionable clothes and the interiors in which the pictures were taken. Did aristocratic people really live in such places?

The faces of the women, and sometimes the men, fascinated me. Since my entry into the film-making world I had discovered a good deal about how make-up and costume could alter someone's appearance, but it was still astonishing to see how the camera captured something that was not real. Although the caption on the photograph reported the person's name, and often their parentage, their faces were like ghosts', pale-cheeked and dark-eyed, with a look both haughty and haunting as they posed in silk dresses and rows of pearls. It reminded me how little of me – the real person – the cinema audience would ever see. To them I would be as ghostly and two dimensional as these visions in the magazine.

I began a sigh, but it turned into a gasp. I sat forward. "Aidan, look at this!"

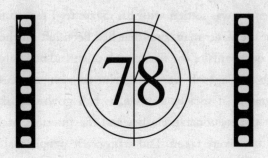

I passed him the open magazine. "That photo, of a party in New York. Look at the names underneath it."

He gazed, blinking, at the page. "Well, would you believe it?" He whistled through his teeth. "She's a beauty, isn't she?"

We looked at the picture together. It was on the society gossip page and featured a smartly dressed couple posing at a charity event at the Waldorf Hotel. The woman, a beauty as Aidan had said, was hand in hand with the man, and both were smiling happily. The caption read: *Among the distinguished guests were Mr Heinrich Stolz, the well-known art collector, and his constant companion, Miss Catherine Melrose, who has recently launched her latest collection of exquisite jewellery.*

But she was not Miss Catherine Melrose. She was Mrs David Penn.

"Good grief, the man must be crackers," said Aidan. "Who would divorce this gorgeous creature for *Marjorie Cunningham*?" Then, after a pause, "Though I suppose darling Marjorie *is* nearer his age."

But I could not dismiss the photograph so glibly. It remained before my eyes all the way to Calais and was still there when we boarded the train to Paris. I tried to sleep; I tried to think of something else. I tried to engage Aidan in conversation. Everything failed to erase it. At Paris we took a taxi to another station, where the sleeper train which would take us through France and Switzerland and on to Italy was waiting. Aidan bought ham rolls, croissants and coffee through the window of the carriage from a little cart that trundled along the platform, and we ate ravenously. The coffee was the best I had ever tasted. When I mentioned this to Aidan, he grinned, raised his cup and said, "There is no such thing as coffee in England, really, you know."

"Or Wales," I added. What would Frank say if he knew what delicious bread, pastries and coffee existed? I resolved at that moment that nothing would stop me from bringing him, and even Mam and Da, to Europe some day. Whatever lay in my future, I could not let this privilege be mine alone.

The train set off; the day wore on. Much of northern France was flat, with lines of trees, and the land was still scarred here and there by the remnants of the war – bumpy fields where trenches had been, and ruined buildings. But as dusk fell, our journey took us towards the Alps, and I glimpsed the distant blue-grey mountains with their white caps. Sleepy as I was, I stared, thrilled by the sight. But even as I did, the scenery faded and Catherine Penhaligon, as her official name must be, once again appeared before me. Blonde, slender, dressed expensively in a shimmering gown, a fur hanging idly from her hand, her neck and ears decorated by diamond jewellery, perhaps of her own design. I could not erase her image.

Our connection from Pisa was late, and by the time Aidan and I climbed down from the train at Castiglioncello, my exhaustion was reflected by his. Shoulders drooping, stumbling against each other, we crossed the platform. Two porters competed for our baggage, babbling incomprehensibly. My heart sank. I had never heard Italian before at such close quarters. This was the language I was supposed to master, "for verisimilitude".

Aidan dismissed one of the men and the other set about putting our luggage on his trolley. We emerged from the station into darkness and the exotic presence of Italy. I will never forget the mildness of the air and the scent of pines that greeted me that night. I had to bite back the observation that it was not like Wales. My comparison between Aberystwyth and Brighton had been met with disdain by David; I had learnt a lesson.

But my impression of that old-fashioned two-seater carriage, and the stony road it travelled on under a black sky sprinkled with stars, was no less vivid for not being able to speak of it. It was mid-April; I had no inkling of the intensity of the heat that would rule my existence before the next few weeks were out. I did not know that everything I had brought in my case, and everything that had been sent poste restante from the Thamesbank Hotel, would be too warm to wear. My habitual costume would become that of the Italian girls: a cotton dress, sandals and a light shawl.

Above the squeak of the carriage wheels and the thud of the horses' shoes, I heard unfamiliar sounds: insects, I supposed, and the chatter of night-time birds. Above me the pines stretched to the sky, scattering the road with their needles. And all around me lay the invisible presence of *newness*.

During that carriage ride, I strained my nerves in an attempt to imprint every sensation on my memory, to relay to those in Haverth, of course, but also to store in my own heart.

The apartment Aidan had rented was on the first floor of an ancient house built around a small, green-tiled courtyard. The key had been left under a chipped plaster model of a cat beside the door. As Aidan fumbled for it in the

211

darkness, I breathed deeply. The scent of flowers was strong. All around me bloomed geraniums, bougainvillea, peonies and many other species I could not name.

Inside, the house was not so fragrant. Its plumbing arrangements were more primitive than I had become accustomed to in London, though the lack of a bath with running water concerned me less than it did Aidan. Unlike in Haverth, the bathroom was inside the building here, and it was not such a trial to bring hot water from the kitchen stove no more than two yards away. The lavatory, which was a lean-to in the courtyard, was shared with the tenants of the flat downstairs. It smelt, rather. I resolved to buy some bleach.

"So…" Aidan opened the door next to the bathroom and peered in. "Yes, this must be your room, the one with the view over the sea. And don't worry, I won't be on the sofa. There are two bedrooms."

"But the other one does not look over the sea?"

"Not according to the landlady. But both my Italian and the telephone line were weak, so don't bet on it."

I nearly reached out to touch his hand, but resisted. "Thank you, Aidan. Thank you so much for bringing me to this place. I shall be a good housekeeper, I promise. I will keep both rooms, and the rest of the apartment, perfectly clean."

"You don't have to," he said, smiling.

"But it would make our story more convincing if we do not employ a maid, wouldn't it?"

"It would."

"Then I shall be the maid," I concluded with satisfaction.

Castiglioncello was as Aidan had described. Fashionable hotels catered for fashionable visitors who walked with their small dogs or small children, or both, by the sea and through the pine-shaded gardens. Flocks of swifts wheeled in the sky and settled on rooftops. Around the bay nestled private villas. Secretive, mostly hidden by greenery, it was only when the sunlight flashed upon their windows that they could be seen. When I asked who lived there, Aidan said simply, "Millionaires."

"Like the director of your film? What's his name again?"

"Giovanni Bassini."

"And how do you know him?"

"Through his son, Stefano. He and I were at school together. They live partly in London and partly in Italy, you see."

He seemed in a loquacious mood, so I continued my

questioning. "So he gave you this part even though you were sacked from *Innocence*?"

"Thanks for reminding me, dearie."

"A pleasure, *dearie*." I was learning to speak to Aidan in a way I had never spoken to anyone else. He had the knack of freeing his conversation from polite restraint while remaining inoffensive.

"Well," he said, "I came out to their place here a couple of years ago for a holiday, and when Giovanni heard I was an actor he said he'd keep me in mind the next time he was casting. I didn't think anything would come of it, as in this business people promise you things all the time, but I received a telephone call from the casting director just after Christmas, so I did a screen test for Giovanni and you know the rest."

Aidan himself could have rented a villa or stayed at one of the expensive hotels. But he had taken the modest apartment for the same reason he wished me to attend Italian lessons. Verisimilitude. Not attracting attention. An ordinary actor and his unmarried female cousin with too much time on her hands. We did not eat in well-appointed restaurants or visit the bathing stations. We were not there for a holiday – Aidan did not need to remind me.

Although we were further south than Lerici, Italy's northwestern coast was exactly as the picture in the book had shown. Every day the air was sweeter, the sun higher, the ocean warmer than the day before. Each morning a cheerful driver called Angelo would arrive to collect Aidan, who would climb into the car, his camera swinging on a strap round his neck, and he and Angelo would roar off, spraying dust and small stones behind them. Aidan was never without his camera. When I questioned this, he asked, "How can anyone not wish to capture this enchanting landscape?"

"But in photographs everything looks *grey*," I protested.

He gave me an exaggeratedly exasperated look. "Spoken like a true philistine, who cannot see art when it is under her nose."

I tried to remonstrate, but his next words silenced me. "What do you think the art director, the cinematographer and the lighting designer do while a film is being made? Sit and eat chocolates? And do you think you are any less riot- ously beautiful on the screen because you appear in tones of *grey*, as you say?"

And then there was the language school itself. Its propri- etor was nothing like Signor Lingo; Signora Carro turned out to be a petite, unassumingly charming woman of about forty who spoke English and French well – she had studied in Paris and London, she said. I was assigned to the begin- ners' conversation class, which took place each morning at eleven o'clock. My fellow students were well-to-do ladies of several nationalities. The wives, I concluded, of the mil- lionaires. We sat in a circle and, guided by Signora Carro and our textbook, began very soon to communicate with one another in almost-recognizable Italian. It was so interesting that I was sorry I would not be there long enough to learn the language properly. But when I asked Aidan how long we *would* be here, he shrugged, smiled sunnily and said, "How long is a piece of string?"

In truth, I did not care. A feeling of predestination had descended upon me in Castiglioncello. Whatever happened would happen. Aidan, Giovanni Bassini, his son Stefano, my dear mam and da, Frank and his framed cells, Florence and her perceptiveness – everyone who had shaped the events of the past few months must play their roles. Italy, I knew without question, would provide a dramatic, perhaps even the *most* dramatic, scene in the story of us all.

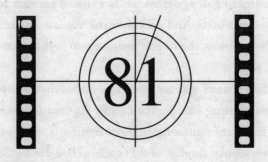

"What if David doesn't come?" I asked Aidan after three weeks had passed with no sign of him.

"He will."

"But what if he *doesn't*? I mean, supposing he's ill, or working on another film, or—"

"Clara, will you stop worrying about things that have

not happened, and may never happen?"

"But that is what worrying is! Once something's happened, there's no point."

He looked at me in exasperation. We were dawdling along the main street, our arms full of loaves of bread and tomatoes and cheese from the market. It was past one o'clock; the sun was getting strong. I had on the hat from which I refused to be separated, and a thin dress. My legs were already so tanned I had no need for stockings. Mam, who was of the generation that favoured pale skin on legs and everywhere else, would stare when she saw them. But Florence and Mary would be delighted. Mary always looked much better when her face caught the sun and her freckles emerged, and she knew it. *She* never wore a sunhat.

"Why are you dreading David's arrival?" asked Aidan accusingly. "Everything will be perfectly all right!"

"Will it? Supposing he doesn't go along with what I suggest? Supposing he's contrite, and falls to his knees or something? You can't predict what he'll do."

"Clara, *stop worrying!*" We had reached the courtyard. Aidan shifted his packages and fumbled in the pocket of his trousers for the key. "Don't think about what David will or won't do, or whether he'll even arrive in the first place. Think about what *you* are going to do, which is much more important. You always show more concern for other people than yourself."

"Yes," I said with a sigh as we began to climb the stairs.

"I have been told that I have a tendency to do that."

"Look." He put the shopping down and reached for his cigarettes. "After lunch we'll do a proper rehearsal, all right?" He searched his pockets for his lighter. "Just like we used to do on *Innocence*. I'll be David, and we'll try to cover every eventuality. Does that make you feel better?"

I did not answer.

"Where the devil's that blessed lighter? Oh, these'll do." He took the kitchen matches from the shelf, lit his cigarette and threw the spent match into the sink. He caught sight of my face and his expression changed. "What's the matter? You're not going to get cold feet at the last minute, are you?"

I was not going to get cold feet. My gratitude to Aidan would not allow it. Into my darkest bewilderment he had shone a light. But his words about being David had struck me. "No, I don't think so. It's just…"

"What *is* it, Clara?" He was not impatient, but his breath had shortened and he was watching my face nervously.

"It's stupid," I confessed. "You'll laugh at me."

"I will not."

"Um ... well, you said that you would be David, but that just seems, you know, odd. You being David. I mean *playing* David."

He went on looking at me, his eyes expressionless. I swallowed and went on.

"You see, I had never known any man before David. No one had ever taken notice of me, and courted me, and bought me things, and so on. And" – embarrassed, I began to slice bread and unwrap cheese – "well, you are a man, Aidan, but you are not David."

I did not look at him. When he spoke, his voice was stifled. "So you are saying that it is difficult for you to imagine me as David."

"Yes, I suppose so."

"Because you are in love with him and you are not in love with me?"

A thick silence fell in the small, old-fashioned kitchen. My heart beat fast. I laid the bread knife on the board, afraid that my hands were trembling too much to cut another slice. I raised my eyes to his. The blank look had been replaced by one so intense I could almost imagine the camera was rolling. Yet it was not Aidan's "acting" look. Something darted through me from my head to my toes, as suddenly as a bullet. Something that warmed me and made my cheeks blaze.

It was unexpectedly difficult to say his name. "Ai…"

I began, then changed my mind and began again. "I only know," I said as steadily as I could, "that if what I felt for David was not love, then I do not know what it was. But I do not know what I feel for you."

His gaze fell, and he took several quick puffs on his cigarette without blowing much smoke out between them. "Is that the honest truth?" he asked.

"That is the honest truth."

"You do not despise me?"

"*Despise* you? Oh…"

My face still felt very hot but, propelled by a feeling stronger than embarrassment, I went and embraced him. He made no attempt to pull me closer to him; he barely even moved, as if he hardly noticed that I was there. But something inside my brain released itself, like a knot untying. I felt my scalp and neck muscles relax. Perhaps the time would come when I *could* do ordinary things again. Perhaps I *would* walk down some street with some man, laughing and talking. I had been unaware of the tension in my body, but now my attention was drawn to my physical presence. It was as if I had opened a door and seen myself standing there in the kitchen, and glimpsed the future.

"If I despised you once," I told him, "that is because I was an ignorant child. Now I am no longer ignorant, and no longer a child, though you must make up your own mind what I am." I stood back and, bashfulness getting the better of me, turned back to my bread and cheese.

"I know what you are, Clara," he said to my back. His voice was low, and full of forgiveness and relief. "You are far too good for me."

A sound like the drone of a thousand bees awakened me, though I barely knew I had been asleep.

Then Aidan's footsteps crossed the courtyard and hurried up the stone stairs. He found me sitting on our narrow balcony, as I did every afternoon when it was too warm to go out walking, and crouched in front of my chair. Through a still-sleepy haze I looked at his sun-touched face and unruly hair. He looked younger than usual, less like an actor and more like an excited boy. I had to stifle the desire to take his face between my hands. "What was that funny noise?" I asked.

"Noise? Oh, never mind about that, that's just my motorcycle. The point is, David's arrived!"

"Oh! Why have you got a motorcycle?"

"Because I'm fed up with waiting for that scoundrel Angelo to drive me around. He's always late, and he's a worse drunkard than I am. But don't you want to hear my news? Giovanni told me today that David and some companions have arrived for a stay at his villa. Stefano, Giovanni's son, is coming from Rome, too, so there is bound to be a party, to which I will be invited. I've mentioned 'my cousin Sarah' to Giovanni on several occasions, and he's always looking out for a nice girl for Stefano, though Stefano wouldn't know a nice girl from a hole in the ground, so I don't think it will be difficult to get you an invitation too."

As he talked, I watched his eyes. "The eyes have it" was the popular phrase to describe good acting, a pun on the pronouncement of a triumphant bill in the House of Commons: "the ayes have it".

Aidan's eyes had more "it" than I had ever seen, except when he was acting. There was a light in them, an alertness, a desire to move ahead and get something done.

"So we have to do it at this party, or never?"

He nodded. "No rehearsals and no script, I'm afraid."

"I'll be so nervous!"

He stood up. In the small balcony space, his body obscured the sun. I could not see his features, but his voice was determined. "Tell me something, Clara. Do you think you could learn to ride a motorcycle?" He was leaning against the balustrade, arms folded, with the smallest of breezes lifting the forelock of his hair. There was a question in his eyes, but excitement too.

"As a matter of fact," I told him, "I can already."

He was very surprised. "Really?" he asked eagerly. "That's wonderful! But how come a girl ... well, you know..."

"Because of my brother," I told him. "My film-mad, motor-car mad brother."

Aidan was interested. He sat down on the floor in the narrow space, braced his feet against the house wall and lit a cigarette. "So he had a motorcycle, did he?"

"No!" I tried not to sound scornful of the idea. "He had a bicycle. But one day during the war, when he was about twelve, a soldier stopped at the Lamb and Flag for a drink of water. All the boys wanted a ride on his motorcycle, of course. The poor soldier had to fight them off. And ever since that day, Frank went on and on about getting a motorcycle."

"And he never did?"

I shook my head. "But he did rent one. He *said* Bobby Pritchard's father let him borrow his motorcycle, but I knew money had changed hands." I paused, remembering. "It was an ex-army 1915 Triumph Model H."

Aidan laughed. "Not many girls know things like that! So did you ride it too?"

"Of course. I told Frank if he didn't let me, I'd tell Mam and Da that he was paying Mr Pritchard out of the money he got from Da for doing farm chores and was supposed to be saving."

"And how did it feel to ride a motorcycle?"

Vivid memories arose. After repeated attempts to start the motorcycle and hot-faced frustration, the machine had begun to respond under my hands and feet. I'd flown down the hill with Frank running after me, screeching. "Marvellous," I said.

"What happened then?" asked Aidan, reaching up to tip ash over the balcony. "Did you get goggles and a scarf, and roar round the village like a lion on two wheels?"

"Well, I rode the motorcycle enough times to understand what to do and what not to do. But the following year Mr Pritchard's business hit a bad patch and he sold the Triumph, and that was that. I hadn't even thought about it for years."

Aidan was still looking amused. In that moment he seemed more carefree than I had ever seen him. His longed-for opportunity to atone for his mother's unhappiness was near. The plan hatched that day on a bench in Hyde Park was at last underway. Now David had arrived, there was no turning back.

I got to my feet. "The clapperboard's come down, Aidan, hasn't it?"

Giovanni Bassini's villa was exactly as anyone would imagine an Italian film director's villa to be. It occupied a high spot, with a sea view on three sides. It had a shady verandah and a sunny garden. The floors were marble and the ceilings heavily decorated. Tall glass doors opened from the ballroom onto a terrace, where the dancing continued. Parked on the driveway was a line of sleek cars. Lights hung in the trees; waiters scurried about with trays of champagne. A year ago I would have been astounded by the opulence, but when Aidan and I stepped out of the car to be welcomed by Giovanni's butler, the only surprising thing was how unsurprised I felt.

It was as staged as a film set, and I had seen enough film sets to be weary of them. I had no desire to see what the women were wearing, or which man was or was not attractive, or how expensive anyone's jewels were. I was so tense that the headache that had started at the back of my head before we left the apartment was now creeping over my entire skull. And I was uncomfortable in the gown that

Aidan had picked out for me from a shop in Castiglioncello.

"I don't like it," I had protested. "It shows too much of my legs. And it's too low in the back. What will I wear underneath it?"

"Very little," Aidan had said. "But it doesn't matter whether *you* like it. *David's* got to like it." I had on a pair of French knickers, with suspenders and stockings, but nothing else under the dress, which was made of thin knitted silk. The straps were so narrow I worried that at any time they would fall off my shoulders, and the skirt was so short, I resolved not to sit down for the whole evening. I clasped my evening bag to my chest as I followed Aidan into the party, feeling exposed as never before.

Aidan took hold of my arm and we crossed the room, ducking between dancing couples until we reached the open doors to the terrace. But before we could take another step, Aidan was stopped by a young man. "Allan, no, I should say *Aidan*! There you are!" he exclaimed, greeting Aidan with an Italian-style embrace.

Stefano was undoubtedly handsome, but I did not find myself attracted to him. He was slim, and about the same height as Aidan, but there were grey shadows under his rather puffy eyes, and he did not have the bearing of his school friend. When his dark eyes rested upon my face, they took on a predictable expression. "And this must be *la cugina*!"

"Indeed," said Aidan, a little stiffly, as if I were really his young cousin. "Stefano Bassini, Sarah Freebody."

Breathing down his nose with a sort of satisfied sigh, Stefano took my hand and kissed it. "Who would have thought that Aidan has such a beauty in his family?"

I responded with a shy smile, though I was wearily familiar with the look on Stefano's face. "Pleased to meet you, Signor Bassini."

"Oh, call me Stef!" He pulled my hand to his chest and held it there. "Signorina, I have a question for you. Tell me, have you ever considered a career in pictures? My father could get you a part tomorrow, just like that!"

I was ready with the story Aidan and I had rehearsed. "Oh no, not at all! Er … thank you very much, but I am training to be a teacher of languages."

He still did not release my hand. "So your loveliness will be visible only to your students?"

I said nothing, but lowered my eyes modestly. When I looked up again I was just in time to see Stefano and

Aidan exchange a "what can you do?" look. My pretence of being a bluestocking when I was dressed, made up and bejewelled like a screen siren was laughable enough, but Stefano's lasciviousness was even more absurd. "I must get you a drink," he was saying, rubbing my fingers between his own. He barked in Italian at a uniformed manservant, who hurried away. "Paulo will bring some of my father's special champagne," continued Stefano. "Only the best for my dear friend and his lovely cousin!"

"Gio is very generous," said Aidan politely.

Stefano continued to study me. "Why have I not met you before? I have known Aidan since we were boys."

Again, we were ready with our story. "Sarah and her family have been living in Canada for some years," explained Aidan. He had assured me Stefano would not be able to tell a Welsh accent from a Canadian one, and the place where I had ostensibly lived had to be far enough away for Aidan's cousin never to have turned up at a school event. "They have only been back six months."

"And what is the signorina doing in Castiglioncello?" Stefano asked, still caressing my hand.

"Learning Italian, and keeping house for Aidan," I replied.

Stefano's gaze travelled lazily to Aidan. "Keeping house? So that is what they're calling it these days, is it?"

"Stefano!" chided Aidan. "Sarah is my cousin, remember. And she's very young. This is her first trip away from her parents."

Stefano's dark eyes were still fixed on me. I could not look at Aidan, but his words had hinted that he expected me to put the next stage of our plan into action. "I may be young," I said to Stefano, hoping my expression was as innocent as I intended, "but Aidan is so old-fashioned, he treats me as if I were a child. You are not old-fashioned, are you, Stef?"

His face relaxed, though he did not quite smile, and he looked down at me benevolently. "That depends on what you mean by old-fashioned. I suppose I am old-fashioned in that I believe an exquisite little thing like you should be with a man who appreciates her." The expression in his eyes intensified, and he lowered his face towards mine. "It must be lonely for you when Aidan is working. Will you allow me to show you our little town of Castiglioncello? And perhaps we could have a drive to the countryside?"

"That would be lovely," I said appreciatively. "You are very kind."

He turned to Aidan. "You do not object to that, do you?"

"Not at all," replied Aidan lightly. "I would rather Sarah were with you than some stranger."

Stefano smiled widely and bowed, and at that moment Paulo arrived with the champagne. When we had taken sips and made approving noises, Aidan again took up the conversation. "Oh, Stef," he said, as if it had just occurred to him, "there's someone I'd love to introduce to Sarah, and I think he's one of Gio's set. Do you know if David Penn is here?"

Stefano was surprised. "But I understood you and David Penn are not on good terms, since..." Not being sure how much *la cugina* knew, he had to content himself with a meaningful glance at Aidan.

"Quite right. We got into a fight," said Aidan, his glass at his lips. "It was hilarious, actually."

Stefano looked unconvinced, so I laid my hand on his arm. "It's all right, Stef, they won't attack each other in your father's house, and actually, I'm dying to meet David Penn."

"I believe he has been invited tonight." Stefano's smile was forced. "Perhaps we shall run across him this evening. Will you dance, signorina?"

"I'd love to." I nudged Aidan. "Come on, slowcoach, ask one of these girls!"

But Aidan had extracted the information he wanted.

"Actually, I think I'll go and seek out Gio. Are there canapés on the terrace?"

"Aidan, you're being very boring!" I told him.

Stefano was beaming. "If you would rather eat canapés and speak to my father than dance with a beautiful girl, that is up to you," he said to Aidan, "but I cannot understand it." He took the champagne glass from my fingers, set it down and held out his arm. "Now, my dear Sarah, I'm sure you know this American dance, the Charleston?"

He soon discovered I was not a practised dancer, so he gave up trying to do the Charleston or any other dance, and merely held me close and steered me backwards between the other couples. I allowed him to put his cheek close to mine and whisper in Italian for a few minutes. Then, when I judged he was off his guard, I raised my voice above the music. "I do wish Aidan were more adventurous, don't you?"

Stefano spoke carefully, as if choosing his words. "He was pretty adventurous when we were at school, you know. I don't know how many times I got into trouble because of him."

"What did he do?"

"Oh, smoking, drinking, going to places that were out of bounds."

I laughed, "Well, he still does that! The smoking and the drinking, I mean. But for someone who works in such a glamorous business, he's so *dull*. Did you know he

231

absolutely refuses to take cocaine even though everyone he knows does? I said I bet he could get some from someone on his film – I'd love to try it – but he refused, and he was so grumpy, Stef. I sometimes think he just doesn't want to have fun."

We danced in silence while Stefano pondered this. My heart was fluttering a little. This was the part of what Aidan and I had planned that was most likely to go wrong. And Aidan was not here to help me or give me cues.

"Perhaps Aidan is conscious of your parents' disapproval. You are, as he has told me, very young."

"I'm eighteen!" I exclaimed. "And even if my mother does think things like champagne and cocaine the work of the devil, she's in England, and we're here!"

"What do you know about cocaine?" he asked. He was smiling, but his eyes were wary.

"People take it to give themselves a kick, don't they? Aidan says David Penn takes it. Is that true? I would *love* to know what that kick feels like."

"And you are not afraid to try it?"

I looked straight at him. "No, not at all."

We danced until we were hot, then Stefano suggested we go out onto the terrace to get some air. "And some more champagne, of course," he added.

"And canapés?"

"Naturally, if Aidan has not eaten them all."

The terrace, lit by strings of lanterns, was high above the bay. Stefano took two glasses from a passing waiter's tray and led me to the parapet. Far below, the lights of Castiglioncello followed the coast like a diamond necklace. I breathed the warm air and smiled at Stefano over the rim of my wineglass. "This place is so beautiful! How lucky you are to live here!"

He did not reply, but leaned against a pillar and looked into my face. "Are you absolutely sure you wish to be a teacher?"

"Yes, I think so."

"But you are unlike any teacher I have ever known. Exquisitely beautiful, as perfect as a china doll, and happy to embrace new experiences such as … your mother would disapprove of, shall we say?"

"My mother," I assured him loftily, "knows very little about me!"

"In truth, I am a little surprised she allowed you to come to Castiglioncello with Aidan at all."

"Oh, don't be!" I told him. "He is her favourite nephew!"

There was a sudden clatter. Stefano looked round, then back at me, half-smiling. "Speaking of her favourite nephew..."

Aidan was being helped up. As he fell he had taken a tablecloth with him, spilling loaded platters and a bowl of punch on the stone floor of the terrace. In the flurry of scurrying waiters and exclaiming guests that followed, Aidan's voice could be heard protesting that he was perfectly all right, that everyone should just carry on, though he felt a bit strange, must be too much champagne, and maybe he had better go.

"Stef, my good fellow!" he cried as we approached. "Will you take care of Sarah? Put her in a car after the party?" He leaned against the wreck of the table, breathing noisily. "I feel a bit peculiar." He loosened his tie. "Seems warmer out here than it did indoors."

I felt his forehead. "Aidan, you're terribly hot! You must be ill. Come on, let's go home."

"Not at all, wouldn't dream of it. You stay here with Stef and have a good time. One of Gio's people will take me back."

"Are you sure?"

"Quite sure." He smiled wanly. "You two enjoy your-selves, won't you? Now, where's Paolo?"

The party went on while the night grew darker and darker, until the villa resembled a bright planet in a void of blackness. Below, the lights of the town gradually went out; above, there was no more than a sliver of moon. My headache increased to such an agonizing level that I could no longer concentrate on anything but the pain. Apprehension, energetic dancing and several glasses of champagne made me feel as if I were floating – not in a relaxed way, as one does just prior to sleep, but precariously, on something shifting. My limbs seemed separated from my body, and my brain from my head. And still, even though hours passed and people came and went to and from the ballroom and the terrace, David Penn did not appear.

I did not know what to do. If the party broke up before I managed to see him, it might be a long time before Aidan and I would have such an opportunity again. I tried to gather my wits and make an alternative plan, but in the end I sat down on a velvet-covered chair and allowed my head to fall forwards. I felt defeated.

"I am having a wonderful time, Stefano," I told him, "but I have such a headache! Do you think the party will go on much longer?"

"That depends on what you mean by the party." He surveyed the remaining guests. "Most of these people will go home in the next hour, but some of us – perhaps you wish to join us? – will make a night of it."

"Do you mean stay up all night?" I knew it was important that Aidan had pretended to be ill so that he could leave me here alone, but at the same time I wished he had not. I wished I could go home, take some aspirin and go to sleep. But I had to act my part. I raised my head. "Oh, how exciting! Shall we watch the sun come up?"

"If you like." Stefano scanned the room again, perhaps looking for a particular person. "Now, if you have a headache, don't you think we should get away from this noise? Let's go and see who's in the garden."

He led me through an arched doorway and down some marble steps. We crossed a courtyard with an ornamental fountain in the middle, to a terraced garden with immaculate lawns. The air was warm; people had brought lanterns from the house and hung them in the trees. Their meagre light revealed a different party altogether. The company was mostly composed of men, but there were a few women sitting on the men's laps or on the grass at their feet. Dance music was playing quite loudly, though the band had departed by now. I guessed it must be coming from a gramophone somewhere. One couple was dancing, frantically, ahead of the music. They looked almost manic, the girl shaking her head so violently that her feathered headdress had slipped over one eye. Neither she nor her partner seemed to notice.

Empty glasses and cigarette stubs lay on the lawn. Some people were smoking, and some were doing what looked to me like taking snuff. But the substance before them was not brown, and they did not put it on their hand and apply it to each nostril. It was a white powder, like finely ground sugar, and they sniffed it up their noses by means of tubes of paper.

My heart drummed, worsening my headache. Stefano had brought me out here to join the guests who were going to "make a night of it". Wealthy people looking for a new plaything. People who took cocaine. And then my heart almost stopped. I saw the back of his head – recently barbered, blond – and the instantly identifiable curve of his neck and shoulders. But I was not afraid. In fact, I was excited. At last. At last, David.

He was in his shirt sleeves, with his collar loose and his hair over his forehead, bending over a garden table. A thousand-lira note was rolled up between his fingers and he was sniffing up a line of white powder with solemn attention.

He did not see me, and Stefano, not noticing David either, led me past. We pushed our way through a group of several men and two intoxicated-looking girls. I tried not to care that people were staring at the shortness of my skirt as I sat on a cushion on the grass. Stefano took a twist of paper from his pocket. "If you are ready for a new experience, Sarah, why not try this? It will do your headache good."

He opened the paper. Inside was not the white powder, but something that looked like tobacco. "But I don't smoke," I said.

"Then now is a good time to start," he said patiently. He began to roll some of the substance into a cigarette paper. As I watched, my heart leapt. It was a cigarette paper just like the one that had led me to Aidan. I still had that paper, folded very small, in the corner of my jewellery case. "This is marijuana, or cannabis," Stefano was saying. "It has several names, as it is smoked all over the world." He held the cigarette out to me. "Here, try it. Take it in, hold it and breathe out slowly."

I took the cigarette and put it between my lips, and Stefano lit it. When I drew upon it, my mouth filled with foul-tasting smoke. "Ugh!" I cried, spitting and coughing.

Stefano laughed. He was handing another of the marijuana cigarettes to the girl with the slipped-down headdress. "If your mother could see you now!"

When his attention was elsewhere, I let the cigarette burn down in my hand, only putting it to my lips when he was looking. David could not see me as I had positioned myself deep in shadow, but all the time I watched him from the corner of my eye. He could not sit there all night, I reasoned. Something had to happen.

At last David stood up. As he walked, swaying a little, towards the house, I leaned towards Stefano. "This is not helping my headache," I murmured. "In fact, it's getting worse. I simply must go and get a glass of water. Don't worry, I can go by myself. I won't be long."

I followed David across the courtyard, up the steps and into the now-deserted ballroom. He disappeared for a few minutes to the lavatory. I waited, leaning against one of the stripped tables, my heart like a stone, my head thumping.

When he came back he still did not see me, but sat down on the far side of the room, put his head back, blocked each nostril in turn and inhaled deeply. I approached, my soft-soled party shoes silent on the floor.

"David?" I said, as loudly as my shortage of breath would allow. "Is that really you?"

His head snapped forward and he wiped his hand across his nostrils, sniffing noisily. His face looked unfocused, like two celluloid images placed upon each other. He seemed to be frowning and smiling at the same time, aware that his features were not in his control but too bewildered to rearrange them.

"Jesus Christ!" he blurted. "What the devil are you doing here?"

"It *is* you! Oh, David!"

His face blurred with sudden fury. "What's this about?"

Now I *was* afraid, but I sat beside him, close enough for our knees to touch, and hitched up my short skirt even further. "Listen to me, David. You called me an idiot that night, and you were right, I *was* an idiot. But I've learnt a lot since then."

My heart felt as if it would burst. Comprehension began to come into David's eyes, and for a moment he looked like the David I knew and had loved so desperately. Not angry or full of loathing, or triumphant, but open-hearted, and captivatingly handsome. "How did you get here?" he asked suspiciously, but more calmly.

I could hardly speak. The world whirled about me; I was back in that hotel room, moments before David's betrayal, when he had held me in his arms and I had believed he loved me. Love, as Aidan had pointed out, was not subject to rules or logic. As I sat there in that ridiculous dress, I barely needed to act the part Aidan and I had concocted. David's capacity for entrancing me seemed undimmed. "I... Well, I came on a boat and a train, just like you did," I said lamely.

"And why did you come?"

Why did I come? I decided to tell the truth. "I came to see you again. I heard you were here, and—"

"How did you hear that?"

He wasn't supposed to ask all these questions. He was supposed to fall obediently into the trap Aidan and I were setting. His beautiful eyes looked very blue, and very distrustful. "I met this man, Stefano Bassini, and he said his father was a film director and knew you, and you were coming to stay at his villa. I knew I had to follow you,

David. I can't live without you."

For a moment I thought he was about to do as I had feared – have me thrown out – but then his lips stretched into a thin smile. "Well, here you are, and here I am."

My heart had settled a little, and although my blood still rushed in my ears, I gathered courage. I leaned forward and laced my fingers around the back of his neck.

"David, I know you are married and involved me in those photographs to procure a divorce. I've worked it out about Marjorie, too. But it's no good." I gazed at him imploringly, as conscious of the movements of my lips and eyes as when I was in front of the camera. "I don't care about other women. I can't stay away from you, no matter what's happened between us. I've realized how much I love you. And now I know how much I *desire* you."

He was staring at me, his nostrils flaring a little as he breathed. He was trying to take in what my words meant. I did not know what effect cocaine had on the system or how soon it would wear off, but his countenance had changed again. David the amiable lover, the intelligent schemer, the exacting director, the consummate liar, had been obliterated by a man filled with bright-eyed, brittle excitement. He did not attempt to unclasp my hands, but sat there imprisoned, his gaze fixed on my face. "What are you telling me, Clara?" he asked faintly. "What do you want?"

I put my head on one side and contemplated him, allowing one of my narrow straps to fall off my shoulder. "I can't go on being that silly little girl I was. I want to be famous, David. I don't care about the photographs, or the court case. It'll be good publicity for the picture, as you said. I only care about *you*. I want to be with you, and be your lover, and come to your house, and do all the things film people do. I want to get my name in the newspapers. I want to live while I'm young. I want to be rich and I want to be *happy*."

He took hold of my dress strap and restored it, slowly, to its position on my shoulder. At the touch of his fingers, sorrow for the loss of my first love affair cascaded over me like an ice shower. Afraid I might cry, I hung my head.

"I know a good way to be happy, Clara." He took my chin and lifted my face. "If you are willing."

Tears did come, though they did not fall. I hoped he would interpret them as tears of relief. "Of course. I'd like to go somewhere alone with you," I told him. "Away from

243

all these people." Before he could reply I stood up and tugged at his hand. "I've spent such a boring evening at this party, making up to that tiresome boy, Stefano, in the hope of seeing you. I kept waiting for you to appear here, in the ballroom. But you were in the garden all the time!"

He got up, his eyes fixed on my face. "Stefano Bassini is notorious for … tell me, Clara, did he give you anything?"

I nodded. "Some stuff – I think it's called marijuana. But it didn't do anything. Have you got any of that white powder you were sniffing in the garden?" I began to pull him towards the doors to the terrace. "Can I try some?" The words Aidan had repeated so many times, "get him to the beach, get him to the beach", sounded in my ears, and helped me act out what we had rehearsed. I blinked away the tears. "Come on, let's go down to the beach, and you can show me what to do. Do you like swimming in the dark? I *love* it!"

David's usual perceptiveness and cynicism had been obliterated by the drug. There was a sheen of perspiration on his face, and his eyes looked a very dark blue. "Skinny-dipping?" he asked.

I led him onto the terrace, and round towards the front of the house. I had to get him away as soon as possible, before Stefano came looking for me and my glass of water. "Look, the path's just here."

Aidan had shown me the path that led from the road below Giovanni's villa to the beach on the far curve of the bay. Not many bathers went there, by day or night; it was beyond the rocks, and few visitors to Castiglioncello had the inclination to climb over them. But those villa owners who did not have their own private beach had cut a set of steps which twisted their way steeply down to the cove.

David and I had no light. We had to rely on what spilled over from the blazing villa above, and even that faded as we drew nearer the beach. I stumbled often in my high-heeled shoes, but managed to hang on to David's arm, and at last we reached the pebbles. I collapsed onto my knees, tearing my silk stockings, but did not care. I had only one more thing to do.

Almost blinded by the pain in my head, and unable to see David's face in the darkness anyway, I reached towards him. He grasped my elbows and pulled me up. His body felt hot, just as it had in that hotel room, when he had put his arms around me from behind, and I had wondered if he was ill. What had been in his pocket that day? Had he been planning to return to Le Grenier and "that ghastly set"?

Suddenly, he kissed me.

I had thought about this moment for a long time, wondering if it would ever come, and how I would feel if it did. During sleepless nights I had sat at my bedroom window, contemplating the shifting sea and the black sky. Despite everything, the thought of David's kiss thrilled me still. And yet the thought of being kissed by a man I knew to be vain, unscrupulous and self-seeking repulsed me. There seemed no middle way between these two extremes. Could repulsion be thrilling? If it could, perhaps that explained the popularity of horror films and the ghoulish devotion of Sunday newspaper readers to stories of murder. But despite everything David had done, I longed for the moment to come. And now it had.

I felt nothing. His kiss did not feel like it used to feel; in fact, it felt nothing like a kiss. All I registered was wet lips plastered over mine like sticking-tape. It was neither thrill nor revulsion. I remembered the electric spark that had buzzed through my body when he had taken me in his arms for the first time, but I did not feel it now. The power I had been so afraid would eternally weaken me had itself been weakened. *When he is weak, we will be strong,* Aidan had assured me.

I pushed my hands gently against David's chest, easing my body away. "Have you got some, you know…?" I asked.

His hand went to his pocket, and I heard the crackling of paper. "Here," he said, "sit down."

I sat beside him on the beach. He gave me a thousand-lira note and told me to roll it up, then he held out a piece of silver foil like that in chewing-gum packets, on which was a small pile of the white powder. "Sniff it up one nostril," he instructed.

I bent down, started to roll up the note, but stopped, and held out it to him. "Show me."

Sighing, he rolled the note, put it to his nostril and bent over the powder. And at that moment, Aidan stepped from between the rocks, his camera round his neck and a flash bulb held aloft. Before David could move he had taken a photograph. Then, for good measure, he took another, of David's horrified face, and another, of David's arms looming towards the camera as he tried to wrench it from Aidan's hands.

For the second time, I watched them fight. This time, though, Aidan had the upper hand. On his side he had the darkness, David's drug-addled state, and his faithful accomplice. I picked up the specially sharpened penknife Aidan had tossed beside me on the stones, cut the leather strap of the camera and made off with it, up the path, back to the road and, I hoped, the motorcycle Aidan had left hidden in the trees.

As soon as the buildings of Castiglioncello began to appear on the road, I stopped the motorcycle, turned off the engine and pushed it through the blackness of the early hours. It was hard work; though it wasn't a very big machine, and I had practised pushing it, by the time I wheeled it into the courtyard I was exhausted. The ride had chilled me; the sweater Aidan had left with the motorcycle had been little protection over my thin party dress, and the headache that had plagued me all evening still gripped my skull. All I wished for was a bath and bed. But before I could enter the flat, I had to do what Aidan and I had agreed.

I opened the door of the lavatory we shared with the couple upstairs. It was inconvenient having to come down to the courtyard every time we wished to use it. But for our purposes tonight, it was a godsend. Once I was inside and had shut the door, I was in utter darkness.

The sleeves of Aidan's sweater covered my hands. I shook them back, carefully rewound the film and removed the spool. I had practised this, too, in the dark, twenty or thirty times. Then I took an oilskin packet of the kind fishermen use to store their hooks, pushed the spool of film into one of the compartments and folded the packet. I tied it as securely as I could, climbed onto the lavatory seat, reached up and hid it in the cistern.

Then, trembling with relief, I pushed the motorcycle into the neglected shed behind the building and padlocked it shut. Then, with the key in my hand, I tiptoed up our stairs and into my bedroom. I had not the energy to heat water for a bath. I lay down fully dressed, with the smell of the smoke on Aidan's sweater in my nostrils and the calling of early-morning seagulls in my ears, and fell into a death-like sleep.

I awoke to an empty apartment. I did not need to look at my watch; the height of the sun told me it was too late to go to my Italian class even if I had wished to. I wandered through rooms shaded and striped by the shutters, thinking about Aidan. His plan had been to get away from the beach as fast as he could, negotiating the coastline back to Castiglioncello in the hope that David would not be able to do the same. I imagined David, beside himself with rage, weaving his way up the path to the road. Had he gone back to the villa, collected his car and driven to wherever he was staying, his brain fuzzy, his body grazed from the stony beach where he had struggled with Aidan?

He definitely would not have reported the incident truthfully, if he reported it at all. Perhaps he would explain away his appearance by cursing that madman Aidan Tobias, who had turned up out of nowhere and attacked him *again*! Aidan had impressed upon me the importance of hiding the roll of film and, when they were printed, the photographs. "David Penn's got contacts everywhere," he had explained. "I wouldn't put it past him to get us burgled."

When I had bathed and dressed, I stepped into the white light of mid-morning and crossed the road, intending to visit the bread shop and maybe pick up a punnet of straw-berries from the fruit stall.

But I had hardly reached the opposite pavement when I saw something that brought me to a halt. Aidan, who should be busy on location at this time, was standing on the corner. Hatless, with a cigarette dangling from one hand and his jacket from the other, he gave me a sheepish smile.

"Got the prints," he said. "Got the sack, too. Again."

I bought the bread and strawberries and some pastries, and Aidan and I walked through the bleached streets to our little green-tiled courtyard and up the steps to the apartment. It was cool enough, but Aidan went straight to the bottle of water he had left packed in ice from the ice van that morning and poured us each a glass. "Let's pretend this has got a shot of whisky in it," he said, and we drank.

"May I see the photographs?" I asked impatiently. "How did you get them done so quickly? And, for that matter, why have you been sacked?"

He put down his glass. "Actually, that's all one question and all one answer. I sneaked into the darkroom to develop the photographs instead of getting ready for my scene. Of course, in came the cinematographer, who guards that darkroom as if it were his only child, or possibly his wife, and bawled me out."

"That's hardly enough to *fire* you, though, is it?"

"Ah. Well, I was already on my fifth or sixth warning. You know what I'm like, bored to death with it all. Gio kept letting me off, as I'm a sort of friend, but even he had to give in when the cinematographer, the costume lady, the AD and even the old codger who makes the coffee started to moan about me." He put his hand in the pocket of his jacket and pulled out a white envelope about the size of an ordinary letter. "By the time they'd finished arguing, I'd managed to get these photographs done, so when Gio came and said it was the last straw, I scarpered before they could change their minds."

He laid out the photographs on the table: David about to sniff the cocaine; David holding his hand in front of his face, though not succeeding in hiding it; David lunging at the camera with rage in his eyes. I looked at them, and the world swam. I blinked away the inexplicable tears. "They're perfect, Aidan."

He gathered them and put them back in their envelope. "I wouldn't have got them at all if you hadn't done your bit so superlatively well." He held up the envelope. "Got the negatives in here as well. I'll put them in a bank deposit box."

"Aidan…" I began. There was a confession on my lips; I wasn't sure whether to make it. But even if I regretted it afterwards, I could not be anything but truthful to a man who had bared such painful truths of his own. "About doing my bit superlatively well."

He was puzzled. "Yes?"

"When I was with David, it was strange. It was confusing. It was as if I saw two people."

252

Aidan was frowning, but his eyes willed me to go on.

"I'm not explaining this very well, am I? What I mean is that I wasn't repelled by him. The moment I saw him I remembered how much I ... felt for him."

"And?" said Aidan, still watching me, still frowning.

"And so it wasn't superlative acting or anything. He believed me because the emotion I felt was actually that – emotion. I was even nearly crying. On the beach, when he kissed me, I was sure I'd be repelled. But I wasn't."

Aidan's head went down; his hair flopped over his forehead. Incongruously, I decided he needed to go to the barber. "So you are still in love with him," he said in a small voice. "Is that what you are saying?"

"No, not at all! I just needed to tell you the truth. I was unprepared for the rush of memories and recognition of what he looks like and everything that I felt in that moment. But when he kissed me I felt nothing, Aidan, *nothing*! And then it all came back – the way he duped me, his infidelity, his treatment of your mother, his lies... Please, believe me, my love for him has passed. It's dead."

When Aidan had put the photographs back in his pocket, he waited a few moments in silence. Then he came closer to where I stood by the table. "Clara, are you crying?"

"No, of course not."

I looked up at him. The muscles of his face and neck had tensed, as if he were bracing himself for something. But his eyes were full of tenderness. Hoping he would not see how affected I was, I said, "You told me once that my life has changed too much for me to go back to my Welsh valley and marry a farmer. And it has."

Without speaking, he took me in his arms and held me to his chest, his chin resting on the top of my head. We stayed like that for a long time. Then I drew back and lifted my face, and looked into his. The very first time I had seen him, on the set of the film, I had thought how actorish his face was – sharp-angled, with the intense look so necessary for the screen. And sitting beside me when I had collapsed on his stairs, he had looked at me as if every memory, every thought, the essence of his being was concentrated in that moment. He was careless, it was true, but his carelessness did not carry irresponsibility with it. He knew what was morally right and did it.

He put his cheek on mine. "Clara … please answer me one question," he began, but I put my finger on his lip.

"Shh. I know what you want to ask, and there is no need. I am where I wish to be. I will never go anywhere else unless you want me to."

He kissed me, and I kissed him. It was not like those kisses with David in hotels and taxis, which had been frenzied, guilty, a means to an end. It was like being swept up and kept aloft by a current of feeling. We kissed and kissed. Flies landed on the strawberries and pastries, but we were too preoccupied to brush them away. I could not predict what would happen when David saw the pictures. But today, Aidan and I were safe in our little room, behind the shutters while the sun beat down outside, and the little fountain played in the courtyard, and the world was at peace.

No one tried to burgle us. No one came to the apartment offering money for the photographs. David, it appeared, was waiting for a lawyer in America to send him an important package. He knew when he was beaten.

Aidan spent the next few days photographing Castiglioncello, and using the motorcycle to take his camera further afield too. His intention was to set up a photography business. Photography was the art of the future, he told me. I had promised to go with him, wherever he went, but he gave no clue as to where he, and his business, might be.

Barely a year ago, I had felt myself to be on the threshold of life, poised to make my name as a film actress. I had been convinced the world waited to adore me every bit as slavishly as it adored Gladys Cooper or Lilian Hall-Davis. But now, I was not convinced of anything. I was still on the threshold of life – I had turned nineteen a few weeks ago – but what lay before me?

The feeling of fascination with, and revulsion towards, the world of film-making had not disappeared. In fact, it had grown stronger. What I had told David in the ballroom of Giovanni's villa was the opposite of the truth. I did not want to do what film people did. I had no wish to go to parties at Le Grenier and sniff cocaine and get drunk. I loved the film-making itself, but I did not love the life that went with it. And there seemed no way of avoiding that life. A film star, whatever she might do to prevent it, was of interest to the public and would have to do what the public wanted. She must appear exquisitely dressed at lavish events, conduct romances with other film stars while coyly denying it, and give interviews to women's magazines in which she gave tips on smoothing the complexion and curling the hair. In private, she must endlessly fight off lascivious men offering her their money and their bodies – and the little screws of white powder in their pockets.

I could not do that.

Opening the doors to the balcony, I stood there in full sunlight, watching flocks of swifts circling in the radiant sky. In the distance I heard a rumble, and shaded my eyes. There, trailing a little cloud of dust, was Aidan on the motorcycle, putt-putting down the hill to the town. A wave of affection swept over me. I knew in my heart that if I were to keep my promise, I would have to trust Aidan the way I had trusted David. To be a gentleman. To resist the desire to take advantage of my youth and inexperience. To love me.

I went down to meet him in the courtyard. He dismounted, grinning delightedly, and kissed my cheek.

"Got some great shots," he said, holding up the camera. "The light is absolutely perfect today."

As he said this, the sound of a motor engine made us both turn towards the street, where a small band of boys was collecting around a brand new yellow Bugatti. "At bloody last!" muttered Aidan. "You go upstairs. I'll deal with him."

"Actually, I think I'll stay here."

Aidan's head whipped round, and he gave me one of his stares. "Plucky! You don't change, do you?"

"Why should I?"

David stepped out of the motor car, shooing the children away and adjusting his hat. He was wearing a cream linen suit, white brogues and spats, and carried a cane. No doubt he wished to blend in with the millionaires on this coast. I considered the outfit ridiculous. When he saw us, he raised his straw panama. "So this is where you're hiding, is it, you sly pair?"

"We are neither hiding nor sly," said Aidan matter-of-factly. "And I can only imagine you are visiting us in order to bring Clara a gift."

David sighed. "Same old Tobias." His gaze slid over my face; he seemed nervous. "That depends on whether Clara has a gift for me."

"I have," I said. The situation felt unreal, like a script. "But you must give me yours first."

His nervousness increased. He ran his tongue over his lower lip repeatedly as he stood there in the sunshine, his hands resting one on top of the other on his cane. "Why do you not go inside and fetch yours?" he asked me. "Then we can exchange."

"Clara's gift is not here," said Aidan. He was watching David warily. "If you will accompany us down the street to the bank, I will retrieve it." He took a quick glance at his watch. "They'll be opening in five minutes."

His distrust of David undiminished, he wished to make the exchange in a public place.

"Very well," said David. "Lead the way."

We must have looked an odd trio as we made our way along the tree-lined street. It was after four o'clock, but bright sunlight and dark shadows flickered over a well-dressed man, a girl in a thin cotton dress and a second man, whose unkempt appearance suggested a labourer, or perhaps, in this town, an artist. Though it would be invisible to an onlooker, the girl in the cotton dress held her heart in her mouth and did not dare look at either the scruffily-dressed man or the smart one. This, though no one would guess it, was the crossroads of her nineteen years.

Signor La Manna, the bank manager, led the way to the strongboxes. David and I watched while Aidan opened one and withdrew the white envelope. He nodded towards David, who took a similar envelope, though buff-coloured, from the pocket of his suit jacket.

"Lay it on the table," instructed Aidan.

David did so, and Aidan went to it, checked the contents, and put it back. Then he laid our envelope beside it. I could hardly breathe. This was the moment when David's trustworthiness would be tested. If he tried to make his escape with both envelopes, Signor La Manna would be a witness, and the theft would be a matter for the police.

David must have realized this. He picked up the white envelope, checked it just as Aidan had done, and laid it down again. "Signor La Manna," began Aidan in his most charming voice, "would you be so good as to leave your duties here for a few minutes and accompany me and my party to the beach? We have something we would like you to see."

The procession downhill to the beach was even stranger than the one to the bank. Four figures now, not speaking to, or even looking at, one another. The few sunbathers must have been surprised to see the youngest of the three men gather driftwood into a small pile and spread upon it branches from the dry-as-tinder plants that grew from crevices in the wall. When he stooped, struck a match and lit the kindling, they must have assumed a newly caught fish was about to be cooked and consumed, although nobody seemed dressed for a beach party. But instead, the man who had made the fire threw what looked like two envelopes, a white one and a buff one, into the flames.

All four members of the little expedition waited solemnly while the envelopes and their contents became ashes. The girl poked the embers with a stick, as if to make sure what was burned had truly disappeared. Then they all

261

turned and made their way back up the beach to the town, leaving nothing to show they had been there but a charred patch among the pebbles.

I was sitting on the balcony, devouring the contents of a gossip magazine. Six more months of Italian lessons had made me proficient enough to understand it, and even if some of it was not absolutely clear, pictures need no words.

A scandal had erupted in New York. Roughly translated, the story read: "Mrs David Penn, also known as Miss Catherine Melrose, who has been living in New York since she left her husband in 1918 ..."

I gasped. 1918 was only two years after their wedding.

"... wishes to divorce Mr Penn, the well-known British film director and producer. However, it has come to the notice of this columnist that Mrs Penn's attempts to catch her husband *in flagrante* have backfired, and he is now bringing a counter-suit against her divorce suit."

So it was exactly as Aidan had said. David and his wife,

desperate to divorce so that they could marry other people, had agreed to set up David's "adultery". Thanks to the double standard, photographs of him in bed with a "lover" would not be irrevocably damaging to his reputation. They would also be able to come to a mutually acceptable arrangement about the division of his wealth, with no hard feelings.

Or at least, so she had thought.

I put down the magazine and turned my face to the sun. So David and his wife were still unhappily married, and stuck in the middle of a court case. He and Marjorie were still at Le Grenier, no doubt bed-hopping and cocaine-sniffing exactly as before, though their next port of call, I was sure, would be Southampton. I did not care what they did when they arrived in America. All I knew was that they were far away, and I was here on our tiny balcony, watching the sea changing from pale to darker blue, then to green as the day wore on. Aidan had insisted I rest, with my feet up on a stool, assuring me that he would bring a lobster home for dinner and cook it himself.

Aidan's work as a photographer had come to the notice of the cinematographer on Giovanni's film – the very cinematographer whose outrage at the invasion of his darkroom had hastened Aidan's departure. His name was Alfredo, and he had influence in the world of Italian filmmaking. Within two months, Aidan had sold almost all his pictures and had taken commissions for portraits from several of the millionaires. Alfredo, meanwhile, with his wife,

Giulia, had become such good friends that Aidan and I had asked them to be witnesses at our wedding.

I stretched my limbs and turned back to the magazine. The picture of Catherine Melrose and her Swiss lover was the same one I had seen on the ferry. How long ago that seemed! In those days I had not known a word of Italian. Now I barely spoke anything else, and had easily understood the kindly doctor when he had explained why I had not been bleeding for two months and no longer fitted my waistbands. Our landlady, who like all Italians adored the very idea of babies, insisted we stay in the apartment until we could afford something else, even though her rules stated firmly, "no children or pets".

Maybe someday I will find work. Once the dreaded public appearances associated with *Innocence* were over, I had no wish to be Clara Hope. My short film career lay in a hundred-and-one pieces around me. Now with my new confidence in Italian, perhaps Signora Carro will take me on as a teacher of English. The thought of the citizenry of Castiglioncello speaking English with a Welsh accent makes me smile.

And I'm still smiling as I sit in the sun, my head against a cushion and my hand on my belly. Yesterday I felt the baby move for the first time. A hundred and two pieces of me?

The End

"Nothing else can break the promise to the devil. You must help us or we'll never be free of it."

1910: After the death of her father, Catriona goes to stay with her uncle and cousin Jamie at Drumwithie Castle. And when supernatural forces begin to stir, it is Cat who has the power to reveal the castle's long-hidden truths.

"I saw no one but him, dreaming or waking.
I fell in love so madly, I almost did not recognize it as love.
It was madness and nothing else."

The story of Mary Wollstonecraft and Percy Bysshe
Shelley is one of the most famous love stories of all time –
passionate yet volatile, heart-warming yet heart-breaking –
and the backdrop to the writing of the world-famous novel
Frankenstein.

"Those in search of a good story need look no further."
The Guardian

"A haunting story, beautifully written and rich
in historical detail." *The Bookseller*

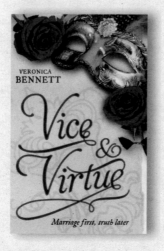

"It is clear you have the attributes required for a secret existence – suspiciousness, distrust, the desire to interrogate, the need for constant confirmation. And you have the wit to think your way out of any situation. You will make a most excellent spy, do you not agree?"

1700: Aurora Eversedge has agreed to marry the ailing but wealthy Edward Francis to make a better life for herself. For a girl with few prospects, marriage to a virtual stranger is only a small sacrifice to make.

But Mr Francis is not all he seems.

And Aurora is the key he's been waiting for to unlock his secret revenge…